The Stranger World of Kim

Short stories to mess with your sanity.

For Linda, whose never ending comments have always
inspired me.

'Kim, your tales are horrible'

It does exist and it's futile of you to try to ignore it, to try to make it go away. You know it exists because at times you actually get a glimpse of it, a sense of it, a tangible feel of it.

Lurking somewhere between here and there it makes itself known to you. Fear. Fear of the unknown, fear of the known. Fear of what you can see, fear of what you can not see.

I get no pleasure in subjecting you to fear.

I lied.

I do.

Contents- (In no particular order of brilliance).

Featuring 'Pop' and 'It never failed to amuse me' and the novelette 'Inculpate' .

1. The Joys of fishing.
2. The Mansion House.
3. Don't listen to Barry's lunatic dad.
4. Call it a car.
5. One What?
6. Nicknames.
7. A Distance.
8. The loneliness of the long distance boater.
9. Harold's late.
10. Two little ducks.
11. Curious curios.
12. Biscuits.
13. No. 31.
14. Random ransoms.
15. The Ungodly hour.
16. Portal.
17. Mums the word.

18. A picture paints a thousand words.
19. Gloria.
20. Gone.
21. Taking steps.
22. Neat furrows.
23. Brendan.
24. Pop.
25. Helter Skelter.
26. It never failed to amaze me.
27. Lady Winsure will see you now.
28. The Movies.
29. Rick's Room.
30. No Cause for Alarm.
31. Over the Garden Fence.
32. Vacuum.
33. Four Days.
34. Not a lot to say.
35. A Long road ahead.
36. Part Time.
37. To have and to…
38. A Flight of fancy.

39.   Inculpate.

The Joys of Fishing

Fifteen minutes past seven he would give it until eight. He was still enjoying the fact that Phil had decided he'd had enough and gone home. Alone he could enjoy the silence and not have to listen to the other man's constant monotonous talk. You either fished or talked, you didn't do both at the same time.

Besides he had one sandwich left and he would finish it before he started packing up his fishing tackle and folded up his canvas seat.

The sudden sound of the duck splashing in the water just to his left startled him and he smiled to himself at the thought that such a small harmless creature could cause him to react so violently.

He bit into his sandwich, his head jerked instantly to one side and bits of semi masticated bread flew from his mouth as spittle.

He had been studying his brightly coloured float drifting undisturbed in the grey waters now his eyes were drawn to the gathering clouds in a darkening sky.

The canvas seat below him fell backwards onto the long wild grass and at the same time he lost his grip on his fishing rod's long thin cork handle. One of his too big boots slid from his leg and painfully stretching the muscle in his upper thigh he made a desperate lunge with his foot to retrieve it. He failed, with the sensation of the colder air now on his unbooted calf the first wave of terror slid up and along his spine.

Flailing his other leg in what now was empty space he inadvertently kicked wildly at the metal frame holding his float collection and bait box and sent it all flying towards the downward sloping river bank.

Another jolting invisible force pulled his head up into an unnatural angle and his futile attempts to fight against it only increased its spiteful determination.

It could not happen but it was, the ground below was distancing itself from him and there was little or nothing he could do to prevent it. He watched as the branches of the trees that had once surrounded him became smaller and less dense until he finally left them below him. He watched as the distant hills that were once hidden to him became clearly visible and real to him.

And now his total inability to see anything other than the sky above his head was all that his mind could comprehend.

A fish out of water.

The Mansion House

We called it the Mansion House which it probably was in its day. It was a vast two storey building that stood glaring accusingly out at the world from the top of a grass and tree covered hill. It was haunted of course. You could tell that just by looking at it, you didn't need to try to enter it to see for yourselves…so why did we?

We wanted to see for ourselves.

The men were working at the back, scaffolding had been erected which reached high up to the first floor roof and disappeared from view from the ground. We chose our day, Sunday, and the men were nowhere to be seen.

And we wanted to see for ourselves.

The three of us soon found the ladder edged against the building's lower wall and it was not much trouble for us to lift it into position.

We were up on the long wooden planks supported by the scaffold peering through the black eyes of the windows and looking at the dark formless shadows looking back at us.

Paint pots and rollers were stacked up beside the narrow wooden door and the short length of frayed rope holding it shut was slack and easy for small fingers to untie.

The door swung open on complaining hinges and what little light had been hiding in the mansion's rooms escaped and left us blinded by the black that rapidly replaced it.

Seeing for ourselves didn't seem such a good idea all of a sudden but the impetus had won its battle over the trepidation.

Three sets of trainer clad feet found their way onto floorboards that echoed our intrusion into a world that until now had done all it could to prevent it.

The impossible silence was overwhelming after the hollow echoing inevitability died down; a cold void of emptiness surrounded three hearts beating in isolation in three completely isolated bodies.

Each alone from the other.

When the apparitions emerged from the corridors and through the open doors the three could only stand in frigid terror and witness what would prove to haunt their minds for years to come..

Disfigured smiles on time ravaged faces hung above emaciated bodies floating on waves of swirling motes of dust. Mingled sounds of voices, words spoken years hence gone unheard, anguished, pained, desperate.

The man holding the ball and made to bounce it on the floorboards but shook his head and changed his mind.

His teammates at his back almost walked into him as he stopped abruptly trying to make sense of the sight that had suddenly appeared before him.

Three small boys running away and screaming in terror jostling each other to get to a small door at the end of the corridor.

The boy struggled to speak, his heart pounding in his chest, he had his back against the safety of a tree and was staring wide eyed at the mansion now in the near distance behind his friends' breathless forms.

'Did you see them?'

His question came to his lips in a series of gasps.

'Did you see them?'

The man with the football bounced it on the floorboards and caught it in his dirty hands.

Home Team Changing Room, Away Team Changing Room.

The men had gone a long way in securing the mansion for their football team's use but they still couldn't keep the bloody kids out.

Don't listen to Barry's Lunatic Dad

The bigger apples were on the trees in the lunatics hospital grounds, everybody knew that. But everybody also knew that at night when the doctors and nurses got fed up with the lunatics constantly screaming and crying -out, they locked them in their ward, bolted the hospital gates and went home.

*

The fence was high but wide gaps in the wire made it easy to climb if you knew where the bigger gaps were, *and we did.* Tuesday night, 11.00 pm Barry said, and bring carrier bags, torches and wet wipes.

David and I did what Barry said because his dad was a famous lunatic.

Barry's dad killed people by putting poison in their tea or coffee and when they were choking and just about ready to die he made neat little rounded holes in their throats with a battery powered Black and Decker drill.

Barry's dad was already in the lunatic hospital and he told Barry that he would tell all the lunatics to leave us alone so we could get as many apples as we wanted and sell them.

11.0clock Tuesday night Barry's dad had written in a note during visiting hours. There were some pears there too, he added.

We didn't know it of course but it was all a nasty trick, a lunatic's kind of trick. Barry told all the lunatics in the hospital ward to pull out their intravenous needles, rip them from the catheters, drop them on the floor and get out of bed. Which is of course exactly what they did, all unsuccessfully trying to stifle lunatic urges to burst out laughing. Barry's dad then turned off all the ward lights and motioned all the lunatics to creep on hands and knees up to the big ward windows and climb out into the gardens. No-one saw Barry's lunatic dad reach under his bed for his battery powered Black and Decker drill; it wouldn't have made any difference if they had of course the batteries were flat.

*

The holes in the wire fence were perfect, just wide enough to get our feet in and enable us to scale the fence. If you ignored the lunatic sounds that filled the cold night air and chilled the blood it was all too easy.

Spurred on by the thought of lots of juicy apples to eat and sell, Barry and us boys dropped from the fence into the hospital grounds.

There were pears too.

*

When the first one struck Barry it hit him with such force it knocked him to the ground sending his torch flying into the long grass. Pips and apple juice poured from the growing bruise on the side of his face and his almost lunatic scream (*Barry's son wasn't a real lunatic even if his dad was*) filled the air.

In an instant the skies were full of flying apples and some pears, thrown by fully fledged lunatics, others by mere *blossoming* lunatics.

The lunatic fighting raged on until the night turned into day and the nurses and doctors returned to open the lunatic hospital gates and usher all the lunatics back into the wards.

We didn't know it of course but it was all a nasty trick.

Barry's lunatic dad had planned it all.

The police report described the scene the next day as looking like an explosion in an apple pie factory.

There were some pears as well.

Call it a car

'How did you manage to get so wet?'

Sally stood back from the door looking in disbelief at the water dripping from my clothes onto the hallway carpet.

She looked over my shoulder at the rain falling in heavy drops onto the gravel of our narrow garden path.

I stepped past her into the house in no real mood to answer her unnecessary question, it was fucking raining hard and there was the car.

We didn't own the small layby at the side of the road, it didn't come with the house but as far as we were concerned it was ours, it always had been, no advantage for anyone else to park in it, the village was a bit of a walk and our house stood outside it largely alone.

'There was a car in the layby, I had to park in the village and bloody walk'

I saw the smile she tried so hard not to smile, before she had the chance to hide it from me.

'Well it's not our layby is it darling'

I ignored her as Wilfred our dog licked me home.

The alarm clock told me it was 5.30 am. Friday, one more day at work and the wedding weekend would be upon us. Breakfast would be a cup of coffee and a good cough, I'd given up smoking over a year ago but it hadn't as yet given me up.

I hoped I hadn't disturbed Sally, Wilfred would do that later when I'd left the house.

*

The rain had stopped but the dark clouds still held the threat of more.
I had totally forgotten the car until I saw it. Sitting in 'our' layby as if it had every right to do so which of course it did.
I tried to console myself with that thought as I pulled my coat together, buttoned it and started the irritating and time consuming walk into the village.
Fucking car.

*

'What's with the sour face Mike?'
It was more than the heavy traffic, and the heavier rain, and sitting in front of my expectant computer in slightly damp clothes, I could think of nothing to smile about.

'I'll get you a coffee' Jenny said and I smiled a guilty smile at her, it wasn't her fault after all, my dour mood.

'Thanks Jenny' I said to her back as she left the office on her errand.

*

The day was long and my thoughts were a million miles away from my work.

When Jenny popped her head around the door to say 'good night' I was just about ready for home.

It's not a long drive but the heavy rush hour traffic made it longer.

The layby was empty.

I indicated yards before I had to, no-one was going to drive into my layby in front of me. I wouldn't let them.

Yes, I did it, why did I feel so elated? I'd parked in the layby a thousand times before.

I turned off the engine and let the silence claim my spot.

She looked radiant, Alison, walking with her arm draped over Ralphs. David turned away from the priest and the altar to watch his soon to be bride shorten the time between him, her and their single life style.

I felt Sally's eyes on me and wondered not for the first time if she could read my thoughts.

The service was mercifully short and we had a new daughter in law.

*

Early Sunday morning, David and Alison 35,000 ft in the air on their way to Mexico, Ralph and his wife Lillian probably at home nursing huge hangovers and Sally and I digesting our hotel early morning fry ups driving home.

And the fucking car was there.

In our layby, cold, proud, mocking.

Sally, who never swears mouthed 'shit' as I drove reluctantly passed it, eyes briefly searching its interior for any sign of its driver.

I would have a closer look once we had parked in the village and lugged our suitcase back.

It proved to be empty and no sign anywhere of its owner.

Ignore it.

Wilfred was happy to see us and his wagging tail seemed to dispel any further thoughts of the alien in our layby into obscurity. He could smell his bit of black pudding nestled in tissue paper in Sallys handbag.

I hardly managed to unhook the lead from its place in the kitchen cupboard before Wilfred bounded into the back of my legs.

'Walkies' called out Sally from her chair in the lounge. She loved to tease me, walking Wilfred at night was my job. Walking Wilfred any time of the day was my job.

It was cold, dark and drizzling. I had to rub my eyes to focus properly but on nearing the layby I still had to squint to assure myself of the sight before me, the layby was empty. Empty.

Wilfreds walk tonight would end early at the railway bridge over the village's high street and we would both be travelling back in the car, but not before I'd had a quick pint and Wifred had licked a bag of crisps into oblivion.

Stop rushing your pint Mike, for god's sake what's your hurry?

I knew what my 'hurry' was.

To get back to the layby and get the car parked before…

It was there. Parked neatly in '*my fucking layby*'
I had no choice but to drive back into the village, my hands gripping the steering wheel and a bursting bladder.

*

Vauxhall Corsa, 1400 Reg EO54 YUN. Sally looked over the rim of her wine glass at me, Wilfred had sensed my mood and was lying in the doorway of the kitchen, head between his paws.
'So you've memorised the car's details, what can you do about it Mike' ?
I'd already thought about Sallys question and realized there was fuck all I could do about it. All legit, above board, all innocent, anybody with a car could park it there.
It didn't matter though because tomorrow the nuisance car would be gone, the layby empty and I would never see it again.

And I was right about one thing, the next day there was no sign of it.

*

'Wear the red jersey, it looks comfortable on you'
Sally was sitting on the bed finishing her makeup, Wilfred was making clicking noises with his claws on the stone tiles of the landing, well aware that he would soon be alone in the house.
'I hope we don't have to sit for hours looking at snaps of their honeymoon in Mexico'
Sally told me to shut up and not to be such a miserable bastard, of course David and Alison will want us to see their photos.
Get a move on or we'll be late.
My mood was light actually, it was Sally's turn to drive.

*

The weather was warm, it was only just getting dark and our car a short walk from the front door parked in, what was our layby again. We hadn't seen the Corsa for days and had almost forgotten it. Almost.

'This was our hotel,The Aquamarina Beach Hotel, Cancun, it was absolutely incredible and where we spent most of our time and David got his sunburn' Alison was giggling and only just stopped herself from patting ours sons still sore arm'
I winced and nearly spilt my wine.
'Looks divine' Sally gushed over her orange juice.

*

It was getting on for 1am and raining quite heavily when we left David and Alison's flat for the hour-long drive home.
'They seem happy together'

Sally told me as she turned up the car's heater.
Nothing more was said.

'I don't fucking believe it'
I must have drifted off in the warmth of the car but the first thing I thought of when Sally's voice shook me awake was her swearing again, which was something she rarely did.
I sat up immediately, yanking the seat belt away from where it had gathered under my chin and followed her gaze through the strokes of the busy windscreen wipers.
We had just drawn level with it when I echoed my wifes words.
'I dont fucking believe it'
The car was sitting in our layby.
'Stop, Sally, stop here'

I was now fully alert and tapping the car's window with my rigid index finger turning back in my seat.

Sally had touched the brakes and was pulling in towards the nearside kerb, she hesitated and then put her foot back on the accelerator.

'Stop here, Sally, stop here'

The words were out of my mouth before I realised I had spoken them.

Sally had taken her eyes from the road and was glaring at me …

'Why, what the hell do you think you are going to do, push the bloody thing out of the way?'

By now we had passed the car and were well on our way into the village.

We would have to park up and walk back to the house, in the heavy rain and getting on for 2.30 am in the morning. Christ.

*

Wilfred knows it's Sunday morning just as well as we do. He knows that as soon as breakfast is over I will go into the cupboard set into the wall of the kitchen and come out with his lead in my hands. He knows that we will walk into the village and I will sit him down outside the newsagents and disappear into it for a short time and come out with a paper in my hand and a chewy treat in my pocket. He does not know my main focus this morning would be whether or not a certain car would be parked in a certain layby. It wasn't.

Wilfred stood from his place on the lounge carpet and made his determined way to the front door, at the sound of the bell we both looked at each with the same surprised look on our faces.
'Didn't expect to find you in, nearly went straight past'

Wilfred was greeting Ian before I had a chance to, his tail a blur at his rear. I opened the door wider when I realised Jenny was standing behind him.

'Hi guys, Sally's voice came from somewhere behind me.

'Come in, come in, nice to see you both' I put my hand down to grab at Wilfreds collar, pulling him back and echoing my wifes words.

'Come in, come in'

Ian and Jenny were never in our house long before the drinks were out and tonight would be no exception.

*

'How'd the wedding go?'

Ian had made himself comfortable on the sofa and Wilfred had finally grown tired of having his ears mashed and trotted over to his place on the carpet to doze.

Sally and Jenny were sitting in the kitchen catching up on all the village's exciting gossip.

'Sorry we couldn't make it but…'

I didn't let him finish.

'I suppose it went ok'

The ensuing silence was pregnant with unspoken words.

It was no secret that myself and Sally were not overly fond of our new daughter-in-law Alison, and for one very good reason.

A man called Tony.

*

'So what have you done with the old car, sold it, getting a new one?, Didn't see it in your layby on our way down'

Your layby

I was happy that Ian had changed the subject but I took a big gulp of red wine before I spoke.

I then surprised myself with my own answer, maybe I was slowly beginning to believe it was the correct one.

'S'not our layby mate, anyone can park there, you know that'

He was holding his empty glass out to me for a top up.

'Of course it's your layby, why would anybody else park there? It's a bloody long walk into the village so…'

'Oh you're not on about that bloody layby again are you Mike'

It was Sally, she and Jenny were joining us in the lounge.

I shot my wife a frowned look that said.

'*You are as pissed off with that bloody car in the layby just as much as I am.*

The atmosphere in the house cooled slightly and everybody felt it, so I had to do something about it.

'How's your Josh, Jenny, still enjoying University?'

That did the trick, the conversation flowed easily as it always did with our old friends and before anyone really noticed it was almost 01.30 and Jenny was being helped from the dent she had made in our sofa by Ian's helping hand.

'Better be off guys, Ian almost staggered as he got to his feet with Jenny hanging on to his arm.

'Pissed again' he said to a chorus of laughter from us all.

'Our place next time'.

Wilfred raised his head to watch them go but made no attempt to stand.

We were tidying up in the kitchen, surprised at how many empty wine bottles were cluttering up the work surfaces when my mobile went off.

Ian.

Your layby is not empty now mate, there's a car in it.

A Vauxhall Corsa, thanks for a great
evening.

*

If a dog could look surprised it would look
like Wilfred did when I took his lead out of
its place in the cupboard and walked
towards him with it.
'Mike, where the hell are you going at this
time of night?'
'Need to get some air'
'You're going to see if that car is in the
layby aren't you?'
'No' I lied.
'For Christ sake it's nearly 2 in the
morning, what the hell do you think you
are going to do?'
It was too late, Wilfred had got the sense
of an extra walk and it would have been
cruel to deny him.
That was my thinking through a red wine
haze and it was good enough.

Sally's huge sigh said it all, I heard it as the door closed behind me and the cold night air stung my cheeks.

'What the hell do you think you are going to do?'

Sally's words echoed in my brain as I was dragged up the road by a determined and so much more sober cocker spaniel.

Tony

'His name is Tony and he works in an office a few offices down from mine'

'You don't have to explain anything to me Alison, it's none of my business'

The coffee was cold and my wet trousers were sticking uncomfortably to my legs.The small plastic and metal chair I was sitting in compounded the unhappy situation.

'I've worked with him for ages, we're just old friends really'

Old friends that sit in a car in the park late into the night obviously engaged in a sexual activity.

If Wilfred hadn't been so inquisitive I would never have seen them.

I took my eyes from hers and looked at the chalk written menu on the wall of the dowdy cafe…

Chips with everything.

I wouldn't have been in there if it wasn't raining heavily and a coffee seemed like a good idea.

I didn't expect to see Alison just as she didn't expect to see me that night in the park a few days ago.

'Anyway it's all over now, I'm not seeing him anymore'.

"Glad to hear it as you are marrying my son in a few weeks" I said, noticing that Ham, Egg and Chips are only £5.50.

'There is no need to tell him anything honest, I'm not seeing Tony anymore, we're…'
I didn't tell David anything, he wouldn't believe me anyway, he was well aware that neither I nor his mother had any time for Alison, her having been married twice before.

*

A pale reflection of the moon reflected from a black blind windscreen. The car sat in a surreal silence that was only periodically interrupted by the sound of a passing vehicle. Now and again a curious face appeared illuminated by interior car lights to stare at the crazy man walking his dog.
Ignoring all I walk towards the lonely empty parked car unable to shake the feeling of the complete absurdity of my actions.

'Sally was right, what the hell did I think I was going to do?'

I was standing within touching distance of the car's bonnet, so I did, it was cold.

I put my face as close as I could to a side window and with an open palm against my brow to shade what little light there was I stared into the interior of someone else's property.

On the passenger seat an opened packet of biscuits and from what I could make out in the gloom crumbs spread about.

On the back seat a little person, legs splayed out sitting, unmoving staring at me with blind eyes. A child's doll.

Wilfred was not happy, I felt the lead tighten as he tried to pull me from the edge of the laybys kerb.

Straightening up I looked up and down the dark road.

'Expecting to see what?'

'The cars owner walking towards me eating from a bag of chips, his keys dangling from his greasy fingers…'
The effects of imbibing too much wine no longer clouding my mind, Wilfreds continuous fretting and the cold night becoming colder conspired to make me finally see sense.

When I got back to the house Sally was lying fast asleep on the couch, I laid a blanket over her and made my way as quietly as I could to bed.

*

'Hey, you'
At first I could not see where the voice was coming from and then I could. The car door was opening and the man was stepping out into the layby. My layby.
'Hey, what do you think you are doing'
I hesitated and looked down at my feet, Wilfred was nowhere in sight.

The man was holding out a packet, he was offering me a biscuit. He was walking towards me crunching on a biscuit and grinning crumbs.

'Someone told me this was your layby'

I tried to answer him but my mouth would not work.

'Yeah, someone told me that it was your layby'

The man stopped, turned to one side and gestured to the parked car, the door still open.

'Sorry, shouldn't park there should I?'

'Tony said I shouldn't park there'

The car hooted and the hooting turned into pinging and I slammed my hand down on the off button of the alarming alarm clock.

*

Sally picked the estimate for the third time and sighed for the third time.

'Do you really think it's worth having our drive widened and half of our small garden dug up just to park the car Mike?'
'Yes' I said.

One What ?

So what you're saying is, if I'm hearing you right, this weird and colourless gas is seeping up from the ground and it is getting stronger and stronger and every second it obliterates one word from our sentences.
That's correct, scientists all the world are at this very moment working hard to find a solution, maybe in another gas form or a that we could use to fill the tiny holes from which the gas is escaping.
 I know it sounds really strange and unbelievable but tests have proven that the gas is getting stronger but surely obliterating more and more words.

Wow, this is really freaking people our sentences are getting shorter and every time we speak.
Something to be done about because it be long before no-one understand what people are
A new generation will up not knowing is said to them
We do some this it us crazy.
What do it looks
How?
I

Nicknames

Such are nicknames.
I'd been home only a few hours and a chat with my old schoolmate Tin'ead was well overdue, lots to tell him about Sally Thomas or '*Topsie*' as we called her..
'Mum, just popping up the road to chat to Tin'ead'

'Who?'

'Tin'ead, lives next door to the 'Rowlands'

Mum's face went from blank to pained in a second.

'Oh, you mean Mrs Townsend youngest David'

That was two things I didn't know about Tin'ead, one was his real name was David Townsend and the second thing, he had died.

RIP David.

A Distance

'See if you can find a station that doesn't keep drifting in and out'

Frannie reached for the radio tuner, I flicked a glance up at the road sign as we flashed past it.

Thatcham 17 miles.

'Shouldn't be long now, I hope Dave and Cloe are ready'

'This will do,' Frannie said over the Eurythmics singing about a missing angel.

I reached into the glove box and took two wine gums from the almost empty packet.

'Here' Frannie took one from my hand and popped it in her mouth.

A little drizzle spread itself over our already smeared windscreen, I dipped the wiper blade lever in time to just catch sight of another road sign.

Thatcham 17 miles. I must've misread the last one.

'I hope that annoying John bloke isn't going to be there'

Frannie didn't like John, not many people did.

He's Cloe's brother of course he's going to be there, just ignore him and..

The sign was almost behind us before I saw it.

Thatcham 17 miles.

'Did you see that Frannie?'

'What?'

That sign, and why do you always keep on about John he's an arsehole, nothing to get bothered about.

'Do you think Cloe will be drinking seeing she must be about 4 months gone now?'

I didn't hear Frannie's question.

The sign said.

Thatcham 17 miles, I was sure of it.

'Are we late or something?'

I followed Frannies eyes to the car's dashboard.

65.

I want to see the next one I said to Frannie as if that was an answer to her question.

And then we were at it.

Thatcham 17 miles.

The Loneliness of the Long Distance Boater

The silence was almost total, the only sound interrupting it, the infrequent rasping of the mooring ropes tethered to the boat's onboard mooring pins.

We were sitting in the meagre light from the main cabin's windows reading and hoping the other would get up and switch the overhead cabin lights on.

When Jen finally spoke I thought it was to ask me to do that very thing but it wasn't.

'Tim, we've left the tiller out'.

I closed my book, laid it flat on my lap and looked across the narrow space between us trying to keep the tinge of annoyance out of my voice.

'Christ Jen, we're moored up miles from civilization, not a towpath in sight and you're worried about the tiller?'

I regretted saying it as soon as I did, our tiller was not only made of the obligatory brass but also ornately decorated, with a lion's head, it would be a shame for it to be stolen.

I was being lazy and the wine was clouding my judgement.

'Look love have you seen any other narrow boats since we navigated that last lock, come to that have you seen a living soul since…?

I felt Bodhran gently rock as Jen put her book down on the deck and made to, stand.

I reached over to take her arm in my hand and gently held her back.

'Ok, Ok, I'll go and bring it in.

Her coyish smile said 'I win'.

I made my way past our sleeping berth through the narrow doorway and up the two small steps onto what we called jokingly the 'poop' deck. The aft awning was lowered over the tall metal canopy struts and zipped into place but the tiller in question still protruded through its slot in the heavy waterproof fabric. It was when I was able to stand up to my full height and peer through the transparent plastic 'window' in the awning that I saw the distorted image of it.

The bulk of the narrow boat moored so close to our aft hull that we were almost touching fenders.

With my curiosity piqued I unzipped the land side of the awning and lowering my head slightly stepped out onto the grassy bank and cooling late evening air.

Bodhrun rocked gently as my weight left her and I'm sure Jenny inside the cabin would be immediately aware that I was no longer aboard.

From where I was standing on the bank I could see she was a sixty footer at least, decorated in the garish colours of a traditional canal narrow boat, her mooring ropes frayed with age but tied to the rusted mooring pins sunk into the bank in a manner that told me the person who secured it he knew what he\she was doing.

Alongside just above her gunnels and at aft I could just about make out her name in classic black lettering.

No Name

The voice at my back almost startled me.

'Who is it Tim and why the hell is he moored so close to us ?'

Jenny was leaning through the opened section of the awning and holding her dressing gown tightly at her chest a look of unveiled irritation creasing her features.

The boat called 'No Name' had the whole side of the empty canal to moor up in, room aplenty, so why was she sitting at out aft sharing our claimed waters.

I felt my fingers tighten around the shaft of the tiller as I pulled it from the rudder shaft.

*

We were back in the cabin, tiller in its place in the bracket on the wall and I was pulling my old barbour from the small closet area. Jenny handed me my boots, I was to approach our new neighbours in a friendly manner, maybe they needed help or maybe just company. No point in antagonising them but I couldn't shift the feeling that I'm sure Jenny shared with me of a deep foreboding and for no real reason at all.

*

The day's light had bled into the darkening clouds with an unnerving speed and had taken with it what little warmth there had been in the air.
I was standing on the long grass of the mud- soft bank looking in turn at Jenny

standing on Bodhrans aft and the shadowed hulk that was the 'No Name' She gestured me forward by pointing a finger at the boat's closed bow cabin door..

Why was I standing still at all, why the hesitation ?

The dull light that emanated from somewhere behind what looked like netting at the boat's window was flicking and obviously from a candle. Pulling the collar of my barbour up around my neck I took a few tentative steps towards the boat..

I had been approaching the crafts bow, the voice came from 60 ft away at the stern.

'Can I 'elp ya with sommet, Mr ?'

It was an old voice spoken through an old grey beard and carried strident in the near total silence.

The urge in me was to say in response
'Yes, pull up your mooring pins and sail
off down the cut to moor somewhere else
but I bit my tongue and the words I did
utter came as if from nowhere.
'It's getting colder,I think we could be in a
frost by morning'
I could sense Jenny behind me raising
her eyebrows and giving me one of her
impatient and incredulous looks.
'Ya don't want owt, an ee don't want owt
so leave me be'
The voice came again and I realised that
the voice's owner was leaning over the
boat's gunnel with what looked like the
broken end of a bargepole resting
between his arms.
I didn't realise Jenny had left Bodhran
until I sensed her standing at my side,
her breath coming in heavy pants as if
she'd been running.

'Look, friend, why have you moored up so close to us when there are plenty of places further up the cut..'

Jenny was not one for mincing her words but on this occasion she never got to finish them.

The old bearded man was speaking again.

'I'll lay our boat against wherever Anguilla demands of me'

When his impossibly loud cackling laughter bounced off the canal's black rippling surface it caught us both by surprise and stunned us into silence.

'And then his laughing stopped abruptly and the bearded man's eyes stared intently at the side window of his boat. It was a moment before I realised that the candle light that had glimmered therein was now out and the boat was in total darkness.

'See how No Name rocks in the waters
?,' the bearded man whispered under his
breath, holding the broken bargepole up
and pointing it towards the black opaque
window .
'Look what you've done now you have
disturbed her'
Someone was obviously walking across
the lower decks of the boat No Name,
causing it to rock it to the weight
displacements as whoever it was were
making their way to the stern, to the open
door at the old man's back.
When the tall bone thin woman finally
made herself visible from the depths of
the boat both Jenny and I gasped
involuntarily.
Her long grey hair flowed over her
humped back almost to her feet, her
arms were bare from ragged holes at her
shoulders and her spindly gnarled fingers
looked to taste the air as does a snake's

tongue. She was crawling over the boat's gunnel in a fluid movement and darting looks from one side of the canal to the other as if seeking predators hidden in the dense dark foliage of the distant banks. And then all of a sudden as if assured there were none she turned her head, tilted it slightly and trained two black empty eye sockets directly at us.

'Look what you've done now, you've disturbed her'

The old man was talking again but now he was standing no more than a few feet away and talking on a stream of foul smelling rancid breath.

'She will want to invite you in now you know that don't you ? Anguilla will invite you in now, just like the others'

And then we were inside the boat called No Name.

*

'Light the candle, you silly old man, light the candle, our guests cannot see their hands in front of their faces'

I could barely make out Jenny's features in the dull light but I could see she was struggling as much as I was to draw breath in the cloying stench. I felt her hand reaching for mine and heard a faint sob escape her lips and then she was whispering.

'Tim, please, I don't want to be in here'

A movement in the shadows and a voice from somewhere above our heads.

'Tut tut, where are your manners, old man? get the wine, hurry along get the wine'

'Yes, Anguilla my love of course'

*

The light hurt my eyes and I pulled the sheets up and over my head.

Jenny was standing over me pulling the curtain across from the galleys window, a cup of steaming tea in her hand.

I nearly bumped into her as I hurriedly made my way up the two steps onto Bodhrans poop deck.

I could just make out her angry words as I jerked down the zip of the boats awning

'Tim, what the bloody hell..?'

Out onto the cold grass of the canals bank and no sign of any narrow boat moored anywhere near us.

I could not suppress the tiny giggle that rose in my throat.

And then the unmistakable chugging of an approaching boat came to my ears.

I raised my arm to give it a cheery wave.

In big black letters on its bow as it passed me.

No Name.

Harold's Late

'Harold's late'
Arthur was't behind the bar to hear Mike,
he was probably in the cellar or his little
office getting change or something.
'Have they got it down to rain tomorrow?'
Jack was flicking a beer mat between his
calloused and nicotine stained fingers.
Stuart stood and gestured for us to all
empty our glasses. It was his round.
Arthur must have heard Stuart scraping
his chair against the stone floor because
all of a sudden he was in his place
behind the bar.
The pub door opened and all eyes went
to it, Simon, Arthur's son.
'Harold's late'
Stuart was back at the table placing full
beers in front of us.

Jack put his beer mat flat on the table and closed his fist around his full beer glass.

'Police are saying they have no idea who or why the window was smashed at Aldis, no one took anything'

Simon walked past the table grinning at Stuart.

'Where the hell did you get that fucking 'orrible jumper?'

Jack picked up his beer mat from the table.

'Harold's late'

Someone was playing the fruit machine, its lurid lights danced on the pub's beamed ceiling.

Jack dropped his bar mat on the floor, swore and bent to pick it up.

Stuart steadied the table as Jack bumped his shoulder against it straightening up.

Simon disappeared into the doorway marked Private.

Someone coughed.

'Harolds late'

Elvis Presley sang about suspicious minds and the shadow of a passing bus hung over the curtains before moving off and letting the subdued light back into the bar.

Jack put the beer mat on the table and stood reaching in his pockets for his cigarettes.

'Bet its fucking raining again'

Thump, thump, thump on the dart board.

'You going to the game Saturday?'

Arthur was wiping glasses with a narrow grey and blue tea towel

The cold air from the open door visited but not for long.

'Harolds late'

Andy walked through the door following Jack blowing the last of the smoke from his lungs.

'You heard, Harolds dead.

Five sets of eyes went to the empty chair.

Two Little Ducks

'Hows your Angela enjoying university is'
Three and four, thirty four.
'she still living in Manchester?'
Eight and one, eighty one.
'she loves it there she says she may
even
One and four, fourteen.
'stay there after she graduates, her
boyfriend lives'
Seven and two, seventy two.
'in Manchester, a place called'
On its own number three.
'Failsworth, not far from the university
actually she'
Three and seven, thirty seven.
'says it's quite a nice area, of course Mike
and I'

Two and nine twenty nine.

'wish she would move down here a bit closer'

Unlucky for some, one and three, thirteen.

'to us and the family, our Danny is adamant that

Nine 0, blind Ninety.

'he's staying down south, even if Claire's family is'

Four and six, forty six.

'Scottish' mind you Alan has always said our'

Legs eleven.

'Danny is a bit of a mothers, boy always has'

Eight and nine, eighty nine.

'been, being the youngest in the family and having'

On its own number three.

'had whooping cough when his was only'

Seven and six, seventy six.

'three years old, I'm glad really because he'
All the fives, fifty five.
still needs his mum, did I tell you ? he'
Two little ducks, twenty two.
'and Claire are talking about getting married in'
Six and one, sixty one.
'August, plans are already being made'.
Seven and Three, seventy three.
' tell what date and I'll put it in my diary'
Two and three, twenty three
'the twenty third'
Bingo!

Curious Curio

The dense shadows are slowly lifting and the real sights and sounds of the world are gradually coming back into focus for me. It's easy when I look back to ascertain the beginning of the terror that took over my life but impossible to know when the effects of that terror had me fully in its clutches. With hindsight most things can be explained but there can be no real explanation for what befell me over a year ago.

I will attempt to recount my story and will not blame you at all for turning your eyes from my words before I have finished putting them to paper, I wouldn't blame you at all.

*

It saw me long before I saw it, it sensed me long before I sensed it, looking back that is now abundantly clear to me. As I walked into the rather shabby 'curio shop' as they like to call them nowadays I was almost instantly aware of the object hanging amongst (and completely obliterating) other items on a back wall. At first I did not see the owner of the female voice that came to me from the shadows but then as she approached me and our eyes met I felt as if a contact was made that was always destined to be made.

'Beautiful isn't it?'

Her voice was as thin as everything else about her, her skeletal arms protruding from what could easily be her funeral garb, black and lacy.

'It's a Tanzanian Mask carved from solid ebony and unlike the many shoddy replica's I can personally vouch for its authenticity'.

Again looking back I should have asked her how but something emanating from the tiny woman forbade me to ever question her, besides I and theTanzanian mask had already decided I would buy it.

*

Now, after all this time, I have absolutely no recollection of the lady removing the object from its place on the wall, placing it carefully in a bag and me making the purchase. I can only recall the weight of it thumping against my thigh as I walked and my eagerness to get it home and show it to Abigail.

'It's very heavy Tom'

I remember being slightly disappointed at her insipid reaction to something that I thought of as being rather beautiful.

'Where are we going to put it?'

Again I found myself at a loss at her lack of enthusiasm.

'You don't like it do you?'

I was almost afraid to ask her.

'Yes, of course I do darling, its, its, really lovely, I was just..'

To cut a long story short I hung it up above our open fireplace where the natural light from the window played on its delicately carved contours.

It was in a position where it could observe all. I was happy for it.

It would only be a matter of days before Abbi asked me to move it.

*

'It's just that I think it would look better in the hall'
Abigail had put down the book she was reading and the way she did it told me she had not been reading it at all.
'What's wrong with where it is now?'
'I just think..'
I could feel myself getting irritated.
'Why don't you just come out and say Abigail ? (I always called her Abigail when I was getting annoyed) you don't like it do you? you never did'
Abbi looked down at the book in her lap and then lifted her eyes to mine.
'All I'm asking is Tom is'
I couldn't stop the words tumbling from my mouth..
'For fucks sake Abigail I like it where it is and whats your problem ?'

Her voice came to me in a soft pleading whisper which should have calmed my growing resentment, but it didn't.

'It scares me Tom, it scares me'

Again I was incapable of controlling my irrational anger..

'For Gods sake woman its a piece of wood, a carved lump of fucking ebony, how the hell can a simple..'

Tears were forming in my wife's eyes but that's all they were to me, tears.

'It follows me around the house Tom, it mocks me with its blind black eyes and deep guttural voice'

And now I was laughing, laughing at Abigail's stupid words, how can a piece of wood see, how could it talk?'

'Kill her Tom, the woman, kill her'

The dense shadows are slowly lifting and the real sights and sounds of the world are gradually coming back into focus for me. It's easy when I look back to ascertain the beginning of the terror that took over my life but impossible to know when the effects of that terror had me fully in its clutches.

I have had over three years to reflect on what I have done. I still hear the voice and see the blind eyes watching me, knowing me.

Prison has not been a punishment in most respects, it has been my salvation. Nothing can bring back Abigail but she still lives in my thoughts and always will.

The Tanzanian Ebony mask was destroyed along with everything else in the house fire.

And the old painting of the bearded man the thin lady dressed in all black gave to me on her last visit looks just fine on my prison cell wall.

I don't think my cellmate Doug likes it though.

Biscuits

'Alison, where are the biscuits?'
'They are in the biscuit tin darling'
'The tin is empty'
'Look in the cupboard over the kettle'
'I have, I couldn't see any'
'Ok, the cupboard next to the one by to
the sink'
'Yep, I've looked there too, definitely
none there either'
'I know I bought some, they're not on top
of the bread bin are they ?
'Can't see any'
'Oh, I haven't done something silly like
put them in the fridge have I?'
'I'll have a look'
'Well?'
'No'
'The oven?'
'Nope'

'You'll have to nip to the corner shop'
'It's a bank holiday they'll be closed'
'The supermarkets open, go there'
'It's too far'
'Take the car'
'The car's in the garage for its MOT'
'How about Mary next door, shall I pop round and ask?'
'Harry's on nights'
'Ring Danny, he might have some'
'They are on holiday in Cyprus remember'
'Do you think the Chinese takeaway will have any?
'Don't be silly they wouldn't deliver any even if they did'
'Shall I ring them just in case'
'No'
'Are you positive the tin is empty?'
'I'll have a good root about in my handbag, you never know'
'Any?'

'No'
'What are we going to do Alison?'
'I don't know, I just don't know'

No. 31

I wish he'd stop wanting a paper.
I wish he would do what my dad does
and buy it at Smiths on his way to work.
The gate was high and it was always
closed, the sign said
'Please close the gate'
When I asked Danny he told me that a
madman lived there and they were
worried he might get out.
I got a splinter once getting my hand over
to unlatch it, that high gate.
If he stopped wanting a paper I wouldn't
have to and I'd only have five more in my
bag to do.
And I wouldn't leave the gate unlatched
and let the mad man out.

*

It was closed. I put my bag down on the path like I always had to, so I could stand on tiptoe to unlatch the gate. The gate swung open and I picked up my bag and walked through. I walked towards the 31 and it got bigger as I got nearer. I looked at the large black windows either side of the door and the 31 but as usual all I saw was the reflection of trees against the curtains.

The Guardian with 31 written in black marker on the top I took it out of the bag, five left.

That was when the door swung open and I dropped both paper and bag on the ground.

It was standing in the open doorway as tall as a giant, with a grin on its huge face that split its beard from ear to ear. It wasn't until it raised its arm that I saw the knife.

I left the bag where I had dropped it on the ground with the other papers spilling from it.

I left the gate swinging open and I heard the huge thing with the grinning beard screaming behind me.

*

'It's the paper boy darling, you said you didn't give him a tip this Christmas, now's your chance'

'Give me a break Judy, I'm in the middle of preparing the mince for dinner tonight'

'Bloody hell Dave I'm in the shower'

'Ok,Ok'

Random Ransom

And they had good reason to celebrate, two deals, two packets of the white stuff out of their way and a decent payday, Samatha squeezed Anthony's crutch playfully with one hand and turned the music up with the other.

He'd only taken his eyes off the road to flash her a quick smile and when Anthony looked back at the road the windscreen was full of red lights and a tractor.

Mercedes (his fathers) hit it at just under 60 miles an hour.

That was almost a year ago, the scars and broken bones had healed but the consequences were far from over.

'Get out Anthony, we've given you enough chances, your mother and I will not stand for your behaviour any longer'.

'Abigail watched from her bedroom window as the two of them drove away in the battered van'

Her father would be up soon, in her bedroom, hiding under the bedclothes was all she could do.

*

£20,000 In UsEd noTes Or Your prEcious Kid dIEs.

Dont eVeN THink of GoinG to thE POLicE.

wiLL tel yOu wheRe to LeaVe the Money LAteR.

Maureen read the note again for the umpteenth time, folded it with trembling fingers and placed it back in the oversized envelope. She wiped away a tear with the back of her hand raised her head and through bloodshot eyes stared across the table at Alastair.

'What are we going to do?'

'What we should have done in the first place as soon as we got the first note and go to the police'

Alastair had picked up the envelope and was waving it in front of his wifes face.

'Christ Alastair, they will kill her, they will kill Abby if..'

Maureen was incapable of saying any more, her body convulsed by a sudden spasm of deep sobbing…

'You know what will happen if we pay this..?'

Alastair stood up from the chair knocking it backwards onto the carpet..

'They will demand more, it will never end'

'And if we don't..?'

Maureen buried her head in her arms muffling her voice as she repeated to herself

'And if we don't ?'

Alastair walked to the large oak dresser and picked up an envelope identical to the one still in his hand, he tore it open and began to once again read the words that had already ingrained themselves into his brain.

'Mummy, Daddy, I am so,so sorry, you told me not to come here on my own but I didn't listen. Please do what they ask, I

am so afraid they will kill me. I know they will.

Love, your darling daughter Abigail

It was Alistair's turn to wipe the tears from his eyes.

'Who the hell are these people?'

*

Samatha picked up the almost empty bottle of red wine, she topped up Anthony's glass and then Abigail's, the two women exchanged smiles.

'We should have demanded £50,000' Abigail said as she watched the Merlot swirling in her glass.

'The bastards owe us at least that'

The Ungodly Hour

Someone who knew a lot more about cars than he did told him once that even with a fuel warning light illuminated on the dashboard your car was still alright for another 40 miles or so. Michael wished that, that *someone*, was with him when his car started to stutter, jerk and lose power.

Ahead of him a few yards and on his left his headlights picked out a natural 'layby' formed by overhanging trees and a rough patch of long grass.

Michael veered the car into it and just made it completely off the road as the engine died and the sound of it disappeared into the sudden deafening silence.

'Why oh why didn't I refuel 8 miles back on the M1 when I had the chance?' Because I thought I would easily make it home, because that prick told me...40 miles or so, because I was too fucking lazy to...'

It was a while before Michael realised he was speaking out loud into an empty car but it didn't stop him from slamming his hands on the steering wheel and shouting 'Fuck' at the top of his voice.

His eyes went to the tiny display on the dashboard but he was already painfully aware it was only about 02.30 on that Sunday morning.

'Turn the lights and the heater off or do you want a flat battery as well?'

'Yep, better get used to talking to yourself mate, you could be here...'

He had his hand in his jacket pocket searching for his phone as he spoke, trying desperately to push the thought that was already beginning to force itself into his brain…

No signal, no signal, not out here in the middle of nowhere with the blocking mountains either side of his car.

With a tentative finger he touched the phone's keypad.

No bars, no fucking bars, *think about something else..*

'Yeah sure a car will come along soon, bound to, this bit of road is always jam packed with cars, especially on a Sunday at this godforsaken hour.

Now Michael was even asking himself silent questions.

'Oh well, fuck all I can do about it now, ignore the fact that the inside of the car is becoming colder by the minute and push the seat back and try to get some sleep'.

He was now giving himself some good advice, he would push the seat back and get some sleep.

And if the wet urgent slapping sounds on the passenger side window hadn't sent a startled shock down his spine he would have done just that.

*

The figure of what looked like an old woman, long strands of black hair, bony palms flat against the window, her panting breath fogging up the glass, the look of sheer terror in her darting eyes. The car rocked on its wheels as she tried desperately to gain entrance, her fingers clawing uselessly at the roof and the side of the windscreen ripping off the wipers and tossing them aside into the darkness. Michael sat in stunned silence trying to make sense of the scene playing out before his eyes, the old woman frantically opening her mouth and shutting it in a series of soundless screams.

Michael's brain was racing, trying to comprehend fully what was happening.

'Open the door, open the fucking door, for some reason the old woman can't from the outside'

He was doing it again, talking to himself.

'Look at her face, look at her face, she is terrified, terrified of something out there, let her in quick'

And then he was leaning across the passenger seat, stretching a hand, reaching for the door handle and pressing it down.

Nothing, the door would not budge, try as he might he could not push it open, the realisation then hit him, he couldn't get the door open because the old woman had her whole body weight against it.

'Christ what's going on, what's happening ?'

Michael turned away from the figure at the window and before he had time to think, he had the driver's door open and was stepping out of the car onto the long wet grass, the chill air stinging against his face.

He heard before he saw the figure of the old woman scurrying crablike over the bonnet of his car towards him.

Michael stepped back or she would have collided blindly with him and sent him sprawling to the ground.

In an instant the woman crouched and was in the car laying in a foetal position in the footwell, her head hidden under her arms, her body convulsing wildly.

Michael could do nothing else but stand at the car's open door and stare down at the uninvited guest in total bewilderment.

*

The sudden distant noises brought him instantly to his senses. From somewhere in the dark shadows of the woods at his back came the sound of voices raised in shouts, unfriendly shouts, violent shouts, all of a sudden being inside the car with the doors shut and locked seemed like the best place to be.

The interior light flicked on momentarily and then off as he jumped in and slammed the car door, his eyes went immediately to the inert shapeless form at his feet and then the smell assailed his senses. A cloying rancid smell that took him back to his childhood and the stench of the deep ponds in the heat of high summer where as a child he would fish for frogs and newts.

Michael turned the ignition on long enough to open the windows an inch and was relieved to hear that whoever had been shouting in the woods had obviously moved on.

When the rasping voice came to him it was on a draught of foul odorous breath. 'Thou hast saved me from the men who would see me put to perpetual wink, thou are free of evil are thou not?'

Michael looked down, not entirely sure of what he had just heard from the shape that was beginning to drag itself from the floor of the car.The old woman was talking again as her bony, ashen white face came slowly into view.

'Or am I to suffre an even wors fate in thy hondes?'

No, none of this is happening, I am asleep, it's all a terrible dream or I'm hallucinating and when did I start talking to myself so much?'

The car seat creaked as the woman shifted her position and sat up sending another belch of putrid air up into the confined space.

Michael felt himself pushing back against the driver's side door, the back of his head coming into contact with the cold glass of the window, the face and stink of the woman now inches from his own face.

Deep sunken eyes, an impossible shade of light green, a mouth full of black and decaying teeth and a tongue that sprouted hairs from fleshy crevices on its dry crusty surface.

Was that a smile on her chapped lips or a lascivious grin, could he really feel her skeletal fingers crawling up his thighs towards his groin?'

Pull yourself together man, she is only an old woman for fucks sake, admittedly a crazy one but only a frail old woman.

And then she was speaking again, her eyes now torn from his, her hand raised to point with a gnarled finger out into the dark shadows of surrounding trees.

'Thei hunt for me all ore Pendil hill and woods, thei calle us wicca, thei wante to see us alle afire'

Michael followed her gaze and felt the blood in his veins chill instantly.

Outside his car where there was once a flat country black top road all he could see was a rutted and narrow track that wound through long wild grass and trampled shrubs.

Did he really drive that far off the road? Another movement, another slight rocking of the car the gap between Michael and the old woman decreasing her face too close, close enough for her withered lips to brush lightly at his cheek'

*

'Th're, thth under the heaviest oak, the wicca lies with the sir, committing h'r most evils'

The old woman was at once rigidly upright at the sounds of the voices coming from all around.

Things became no more than a blur for Michael as he struggled to drag his body up from the uncomfortable angle he found himself wedged between the edge of his seat and the car's driver's door.

From somewhere cold air rushed to assail his sweating body sending goosebumps all over his skin and the sound of ear splitting shrieks deafened him to all other noises.

The car rocked violently on its springs, once, twice, three times and then all was still, all was silent, the only sound the pounding of his own racing heart.

The old woman was gone, only the foul scent of her remained and even that was gradually abating.

It was a dream of course, albeit an all too vivid dream.

The trials of the Pendle Witches in 1612 are among the most famous witch trials in England. The twelve accused lived in the area surrounding Pendle Hill. All but two were found guilty and executed at Lancaster Assizes…

'How many more times are you going to read that article Michael, you're becoming

obsessed with it?' You'll be telling me you believe in witchcraft next !'

Michael put the booklet back on the bedside table, turned off the lamp and said goodnight, trying to ignore the faint familiar odour emanating from his now sleeping wife.

Portal

Not only were the tracks covered in long grass and the occasional clump of weeds and stinging nettles, they were also rusted to hell. Some of the sleepers that had been torn up were now no doubt garden features or chopped up firewood. The bricks of the tunnel were crumbling with tufts of vegetation sprouting between them but the main reason Stanley was smiling was because of the location of it all.

The middle of bloody nowhere.

'Good old Stanley, 'he thought, 'I bet a train ain't bothered this tunnel for 20, 30 years'.

Stanley did most of his thinking to himself because Stanley was the only one Stanley had to think for.

It had been raining ever since Stanley had left yet another small unfriendly village in his wake and his long coat was heavy with wet, and cold with the wind. Tonight he would have somewhere to get his head down in the dry calm. Tomorrow Stanley would carry on walking until he got to where he was going to.

Nowhere.

He didn't have to go too far into the black 'portal'- yeah that was the word for it 'portal' Stanley said to himself.

Shaking his head sending a spray of fine droplets of rainwater from his bushy grey beard, Stanley and his Tesco carrier bag carrying his world inside limped slowly from the light and wet of the day into the shadows of the premature night.

Didn't have to go too far into the 'portal' Stanley said to himself again.

*

The silence was dark but dry and windless and Stanley felt a shiver of warmth against his bones. Tonight he would sleep and go back to whatever he could remember of what the world was like when he was a younger man.

When the light lit up the portal Stanley looked into it and smiled. When the train hit him Stanley laughed.

This is what you get when you go into a 'portal' was his last thought.

Mums the word

5 Across…Unrehearsed (9)...Impromptu.
20 Down…European sea (8)...Adriatic. 2

Down…Scottish football great (5,3)…Denis Law. 11 Across…Lowest deck of a ship (5)…Orlap. 1 Down…Top school for girls (7)…Roedean. 3 Down English county (4,3,4)… Tyne and Wear. 4 Across…Obstructs (7)…Impedes. 17 Down… Lingerie item (3)…Bra..8 Down.. Type of biscuit (9)…Garibaldi.
12 Across…Eccentric Individuals (8)…Oddballs. 13 Down…Transylvanian Count (7)…Dracula. 10 Down…The murder of your own mother (9) ..Matricide.
'Dad, dad..see, I told you it had a name'

A picture paints a thousand words

'You must have been about 4, maybe 5' Derek was holding the photograph inches from his face and still needed to squint to see it properly.

'About 4 or 5 is that right Miriam?'
Miriam took the photo from him, looked at it, then him then me'
'You were just 4 darling'
She tapped me gently on the head as she said it.
'Where was it taken mum?' I asked not recognising anything at all in the slightly out of focus photo.
'It was at uncle Raymond's cottage in Thatcham, you...'
Mum didn't get to finish her sentence, dad had taken the photo and was pointing a nicotine stained finger at something I couldn't quite see on it.
'No it wasn't Miriam, that's before he moved to Thatcham, that's Theale, look, the old church where Margaret is buried.
'If you say so Derek'
Mum put the photo on the growing heap on the table and took another one from the old biscuit tin.

'Oh look, our old Vauxhall, it was the first car we ever had'

Dad just glanced at it and gestured mum put it straight on the pile with the rest. I thought he was going to say something but he just raised his eyebrows and looked at me. Mum was busy taking another photo from the tin when she hesitated her hand poised in mid air above the biscuit tin.

'Margaret?' She was looking at dad, her brow furrowed the way it does when she can't remember the name of someone famous or in the papers.

Mum's obvious question hung in the air and just as I thought dad was going to ignore it he answered.

'Margaret, Raymond's first wife' he said 'died of cancer, young'

Mum's hovering hand over the biscuit tin remained hovering as her eyes found dads.

'Raymond hadn't been married before Alice, what are you talking about?'
'I think you'll find he was Miriam'
Dad had his sanctimonious voice on and he wasn't finished.
'And our first car was a Ford'
Time I intervened.
'How about some holiday snaps?' I asked, trying hard to sound enthusiastic.
Mum's hands disappeared into the biscuit tin and she leaned forward to peer over the top of it, I could see she was rifling through the contents, searching.
Dad leant back in his chair and glanced at his watch. He looked as bored as I was beginning to feel.
'Weymouth' mum said as she placed a small pile of photos flat on the table.
'Bognor Regis' dad said, sitting forward and wiping his nose on the sleeve of his cardigan.

I heard/felt mum's heavy sigh and felt the temperature rise a few degrees. I was relieved when a mutual silence filled the room and mum selected a photo from the top of the new pile.

'You spent all of your time in the swimming pool, we had to fight you to get you out'

She held the picture up in front of my face, all blue and shimmering water.

I looked from it and over at dad expecting him to contradict, he said nothing.

Another photo, a shed, or chalet as mum called it; small, all white with blue and red glossy stripes painted in straight lines on it.

'Cosy' mum said.

'Cramped' dad said.

Mum ignored him; she was looking up at something on the ceiling her mind a hundred miles away, when she finally tore herself away from her private reverie she noticed dad had taken a photo from the biscuit tin himself.

'Who's this?'

He held it out for mum to look at.

The man in the photo was huge, he had a bushy beard and from somewhere in the middle of it a large toothy grin.

The man looked vaguely familiar to me as if I'd seen him on a programme on telly, or in a book or magazine.

And then mum did a strange thing which made dad and me jump, she snatched the photo from dad's hand and with determined fingers screwed it up into a tight ball.

She stood up, gathered all the photos together and virtually threw them back into the biscuit tin shouting at dad as she almost ran from the table..

'I thought you told me you'd got rid of them all'

I sat there in stunned silence listening to mum as she ran from the lounge and disappeared up the stairs thumping on every step as she did so.

Dad and I sat staring at each other for what seemed an eternity before I finally found my voice.

'Who was that man in the photo?'

At first I didn't think he'd heard me and then his voice filled the room.

'That man was your real dad and I lied, our first car was an Austin'.

Gloria

'Well, that one was a fucking roaring success'

Gloria said nothing, she had been expecting it from the minute the train pulled out of the station, Derek's explosion, they had been far more frequent of late.

'You could have heard a fucking pin drop'

'Stop swearing'

The carriage was empty, no one to hear but Gloria still hated Derek swearing.

'It's no good we need some new stuff, something original, something that will shock'

'Shock'

'Yes, something loud, big, different, something that will make them jump'

The train was slowing down, Derek hoped no-one was getting on at the next station, Gloria hoped someone was, no-one did.

'We need something that they would talk about on their way home, something that would stay in their minds and give them nightmares'

The train was picking up speed again, Derek was sitting forward rubbing his hands together the way he knew Gloria hated him doing.

'We need to call it a day Derek, you know it, I know it, we're finished Derek and have been for a long while now'

Gloria's voice was as steady as it always was when she spoke the same words. Derek knew it, of course he did, but the train was slowing down again and another station looming.

'I've got it, we argue, that's what we do, we argue, call each other choice names and get louder and louder and more and more violent'

Derek had stopped rubbing his hands together and was clapping them excitedly in the air.

'I can see it all now, it will work Gloria, it will work, a few standard gags and then I take exception to something you say and we build it up from there'

Gloria was silent, she'd heard it all before and the train jerked to a stop.

'I put my hands around your neck and shake your head back and forth, choking you making you make funny gurgling noises'

Derek was sitting on the very edge of his seat, eyes wide open, his hands spread before him like a crabs claws'

'We'll try it Derek, next time we'll try it'

The train was moving again and Gloria's voice was soft, soothing'

Derek patted the big reinforced leather case lying on the seat opposite him and a smile spread across his tear streaked face.

'Yes, we'll try it next time' he said as his fingertips gently traced the gold lettering etched into its well worn surface…..The Supreme Derek and Gloria - A feast of ventriloquism.

Gone

'Come on Dan, your turn to get the coffees'

'I've just seen Josh going into the restroom, he'll get 'em'

'I've just seen Lucy going into the restroom, Josh will be ages'

'Ok,Ok, I'm on it'

'What's wrong with the coffee Matt? You've just been sitting staring at it, thinking about last night, you and Jenny?'

'Reds gone'

'What?'

'Reds gone'

'Who's Red ?'

'Not Red, red'

'What ?'

'Didn't see any brake lights on the way to the office this morning'

'What?'

'No brake lights or any other lights on the backs of cars'

'What ?'

'Did you see any red lights?'

'Christ man what are you on about?'

'Red, its gone'

'Are you ok?'

'Look around the office, Dan, any red ? Look at the fire extinguisher, what colour is it?'

'White'

'Should be red, what about the fire escape sign?'

'White'

'Reds gone Dan'

'I think you need to see someone Matt'

'Reds gone Rich'

'Ouch, bloody stapler'

'What's wrong with Sarah, Dan?'

'Cut her hand on the stapler'

'What colour is her blood Rich?'

'White'

'Reds gone Dan, reds gone Dan.

Taking Steps

It was a warm day, a gentle breeze carried with it the fragrant scents of the multitude of flower beds surrounding Anne's Place a delightful little restaurant across Main street Jamestown.The sound of the bells of St. James Church amplified by the steep cliffs that hemmed in the small city on two sides added to the lazy
 ambience of the beautiful and remote Island.
Sea birds played dive bombers in the circles of rising and falling thermals silhouetted starkly against the cloudless

blue skies. A lone gecko clung limpet-like to the roughly hewed and white washed walls of an old prison building, now empty of the slaves and convicts it once held. Passing the cannon mounted on huge wheels and the Islands museum they made their way laboriously to the foot of the imposing landmark that was part of the Islands rich heritage.

'How many steps are there?'

Jonathan, young, agile, inquisitive.

They were at the foot of Jacob's Ladder craning their necks, staring up at the concrete steps that seemingly disappeared up into the blue sky above them.

'Six hundred and ninety nine and its 600 ft high'

Westbrook, old, infirm, wheelchair bound, hugely knowledgeable as far as the history of the small Island he was born on and had lived all his life on was concerned.

'Wow' exclaimed Jonathan, feeling the sudden urge to climb the steps but held back by the mere fact that it would mean having to leave his grandfather for a time in his wheelchair completely unattended. Westbrook, the memories of his youth and Jacob's Ladder flooding back in vivid pictures in his mind.

*

Grey and blue uniform skirts and long trousers hugging thin scrawny legs and in the distance the echoing sound of the school bells.

Small hands cupped around wide open mouths, excited voices raised high against strong side winds. Footfalls of a hundred school shoes on concrete steps and the sight of the children, their arms and legs draped over the rusting railings as they slid sideways down the ladders steep and treacherous incline. No fear, just wild innocent abandonment.

His old school friends, Sammy, William, Rebecca, Billy, Pamela, Audrey, Eric, Gillie, Laura, names that often came to him in his dreams. Where are they all now? A question he knew the answer to. England, America, Africa and so many other parts of the globe. Gone, gone from the remote Island of St. Helena to seek lives that would be far less restricting. (as did my own Mother all those years ago) Not Westbrooke, no, he would never leave the magical island of his birth.

'Six hundred and ninety nine steps and 600 ft high '

Jonathan was kneeling down, his head level with his grandfathers, one hand on the elderly man's shoulder the other on the dusty tyre of the wheelchair, steadying both.

'Yes' replied Westbrooke, his eyes wandering from top to bottom of the immense monument of his youth standing majestically before them.

'And I have stood on each and every one of those steps, just as I am sure you are about to do my lad'.

At that, Jonathan stood but with one hand still firmly on the wheelchair's arm he glanced down at his grandfather's upturned face and was pleased to see his wide smile.

'Go' said the old man, go and remember with every step you take you will get closer to your family and not further away from me.

Jonathan released his hold on the wheel chair and knelt to apply its brake as his grandfather's encouraging words filled his ears.

'Go on Jonathan, I'll be fine'.

Jonathan approached the first steps of Jacob's Ladder eyes fixed firmly on its summit impossibly high, impossible to resist.

*

Sheer adrenalin took him up the first eighty or so steps and it was only the first gentle nagging of his calf muscles that caused Jonathan to pause in his climbing. Holding on tighter to the ladder's railings than he'd expected he would, the young man turned and was comforted to see his grandfather still on the ground at the base of the ladder where he had left him. He raised an arm to him and was rewarded by a wave back by Westbooke looking no bigger than a beetle and so far down below.

Turning his body once more to the task before him Jonathan continued to take each step one at a time getting gradually higher at each groan of his leg muscles.

Pull yourself together Jonathan, weren't you the only boy who could get to the top of 'Big One', the old oak tree in Prospect Park? Didn't you walk across the narrow crumbling brick ledge over the railway bridge before anyone else? And who clambered up the drainpipe on the side of the maisonettes to rescue a kitten caught in the guttering?
You did.
And didn't Grandad Westbrooke just tell you that he and his school friends climbed Jacobs Ladders as if they were the stairs to the upstairs toilets, day in and day out?
Stop dithering and get on with it.

*

He must be at least half way up, he must be! The summit of the ladder that once looked like it was actually brushing the clouds apart now looked so much more structured, solid. Jonathan paused and arms outstretched grabbed hold on to each side of the railings, turned his back to the concrete steps and sat down heavily on one of them. He would rest his leg muscles and wait for his heartbeat to steady in his chest.

His eyes wandered once again to the earth far below, and between the varied coloured roofs of buildings he could just make out the blurred dot that was his grandfather in his wheelchair.

With its spire reaching high into the air but failing miserably to attain Jonathan's great height the blue grey of St.James Church looked like a childs toy.

Down amongst the various random buildings the narrow roads criss-crossed their way through the city and by turning his head slightly Jonathan could just make them out as they disappeared into the brown/ green that was the edge of the St. Helenian countryside.

*

'Oh, the old Grand of York, he had ten thousand men…'

Jonathan was nearly at the summit of Jacob's Ladder and his spirits had risen with him. He could just make out the faces of people silhouetted against the bright sky standing at the top, some looking down at him, people he had not noticed during his ascent, people that were now speechless and in awe at the vast panorama that lay 600 ft below.

At last, three more steps to take and strangers stepping aside to allow Jonathan access to the narrow gap that led to the viewing platform of Jacob's Ladder, he'd made it but then again he never thought he wouldn't.

Catching his breath Jonathan allowed a few minutes to compose himself before turning to look at the magnificent sights that had awaited him.

On his left the vast spread of the South Atlantic Ocean dotted with splashes of colour that were the myriad of small boats anchored in the bay.

Across from him cliffs identical to the towering cliffs he had just climbed reached up as if conspiring with each other to protect the town lying far below in their midst.

Even the sun had made an appearance burning away the slight mist and raising the temperature enough for Jonathan to remove his jacket.

He would sit for a while and bask in the sun's rays before making his descent, he could for those

minutes think of nowhere on earth he'd rather be.

But all good things must come to an end.

Time to descend and any thoughts he might have had that the *going down* would be easier than the *going up* were soon dispelled.

With both hands on the railings and an uncomfortable unnaturally backward stance to keep from hurtling forwards, balance was paramount.

So much so that it wasn't until he was well over halfway down that Jonathan noticed that the small dot that had been his grandfather and his wheelchair was now nowhere to be seen.

Careful not to quicken his pace Jonathan quickened his pace as a sliver of anxiety crept into his mind.

'He's moved into the shade, of course he has, you don't expect him to sit in the blazing sun all day do you?'

The voice in his head was speaking sense and not allowing panic to take over.

'He had that thick coat on because it was cold that morning and it was far too

*difficult for him to get out of his
wheelchair to take it off'*
Of course, he told himself, Grandad
Westbrooke would be sitting in the shade
of The Sandwich Bar drinking a
cappuccino and chatting up the young
girls behind the counter.
Of course he would.

*

There were now so few steps left below
him that Jonathan for the first time felt
comfortable in releasing his grip on the
ladders railings. He took the last few two
at a time and before he knew it the young
man was finally standing on level ground
amongst a smattering of strangers all
going about their daily business. The
wonderful feeling of achievement he felt
at conquering the mighty Jacobs Ladder
was short lived, a quick glance around
the immediate area and he could find no
sign of his grandfather. The spot where

the old man had previously occupied
looked empty and strangely ominous.
'Excuse me, have you seen an old man
in a wheelchair, he was here a few
minutes ago?'
Jonathan stared at the woman pushing
the child in the buggy, hopeful of seeing a
look of recognition in her features but all
he saw was a brief shake of her head
and a half hearted smile.
'Sorry' she replied as she manoeuvred
the buggy to side step him.
A man, scruffy grey hair, pushing a
rusted bike, a cigarette dangling from sun
baked lips.
'Nah, I ain't seen no-one in no
wheelchair'
Jonathan was calling before he realised
he was, his voice bouncing off the walls
of the surrounding buildings.
'Grandad, Grandad Westbrooke, where
are you?'

*

They were sitting under the shadows on the porch of the hardware shop as they almost always were when the midday sun was at its highest, its hottest.

Ma Yon and her daughter Laura, Saints in the true sense, listening to the man calling but not believing in what they were hearing.

The older woman turned to glance at her daughter, an incredulous look on her weathered features.

'Can't be' was all her daughter said in response and then Ma Yon was standing, walking out of the shadows into the glare of the sun waving her arms to catch the man's attention.

'Can't be' the voice at her back repeated.

*

Despite the small number of people ambling about in front of him the form of the elderly lady emerging from the shadows immediately caught his attention. At first he thought it was just a trick of the light but squinting his eyes he could see that the woman was definitely gesturing to attract his attention.

Jonathan's spirits rose as he began to approached her and a vision of his grandad sitting in the cool lounge of her house eating a slice of bread smothered in 'Bread and Dance'* sprang into his mind.

Drawing closer he saw that there were actually two women now standing in the sun and it was obvious even from the short distance they were mother and daughter and both incredibly old.

'Jonathan, Jonathan?'

The older woman was speaking, her ancient mouth forming words that at first he could not comprehend.

'What is it?'

Again Jonathan heard the words but his mind struggled to understand, this woman speaking was a complete stranger to him.

'You are looking for Westbrooke? You are looking for Westbrooke?

It was the younger of the two women and she had stepped in front of her mother and her partly decayed face now inches from Jonathan's she raised her arm and placed a skeletal hand on his shoulder.

'Westbrooke died over seventy years ago Jonathan' she said.

'Seventy years ago'......remember?'

*Bread and Dance ...A traditional St.Helenian Tomato and Chilli based dish.

Neat Furrows

If it weren't for the colony of gulls squabbling behind me in the cloud of grey diesel exhaust my old Massey Fergusson tractor puffed into the air, I'd have no company at all. Well I know that rabbits and various other small creatures that abound in the field are keeping a wary eye on me but I very seldom see any of them. Which isn't surprising really given the noise from old Betsie's 50 HP engine, even if only about 47 of her horses are still pulling their weight. It's a very lonely life sometimes being a farmer. I started late this morning and experience has told me that this field was a good 8 hours in the ploughing.

With any luck and if Betsie quits her erratic spluttering I should be finished before it gets to twilight.

Wish I hadn't eaten all my grub too early and the tea left in my thermos is colder than a cow's egg.

I'm running my furrows straight and parallel with the main road and it's a good sign that I'm getting closer to the wire and concrete pillar fencing between me and it. 'U' turns at the end of each furrow are getting easier as the earth nearer the road is nowhere near as boggy as it was in the middle of the field. Soon I'll use old Harry as a turning point which in itself tells me my days work is almost at an end, good old Harry.

As kids we'd climb the ancient oak tree, its huge branches wide and low made it easy for even the smallest of us, even the girls.

Once round his enormous trunk and back the way I came a couple more times and I'd be in line to exit through the five barred gate and on the gravel lane back to Clover Farm, my home and a nice hot dinner.

It was on the last circumnavigation of the old Harry that my problem started.

*

K.C. loves L.M. carved in old Harry's bark with my old Swiss army knife, I always made a special effort to lean over the tractor's mud encased tyre to see it. How many years ago? A good few.

The stuttering jerks that suddenly grabbed my attention and tore my eyes from the faded arborglyph shuddered through Betsie's rusting bodywork and felt instantly as if the other 47 horses of her engine had finally seized. The coughed plume of black smoke from the exhaust confirmed it.

I was on the field side of the old oak and half way around it, and therefore the road was obscured from my view, all I could see was old Harry's wide trunk and the high ridges in the earth that were her semi submerged roots.

Betsie's huge tyres were fighting to gain friction against the bumpy ground just as if an invisible and powerful hand had a grip of the plough behind and was trying to pull us back.

And then as I stood up from my metal seat, turned back and glanced over my shoulder I saw them.

Two lengths of thick wire caught on the cutting wheels of the plough.

I put Betsies engine into neutral and got down from the cab to have a closer look.

*

Out of the warm and confined cab the first thing that struck me was how cold it was and the shadows from old Harry's thick branches above my head made everything that much darker.

It was getting late and the last thing I needed was a problem with the plough or Betsie.

With one hand on a huge heavily treaded tyre I steadied myself to take the few steps to where the plough was coupled to the tractor and knelt down to get a better look.

At first all I saw was mud grass and then more mud and grass plastered to the ploughs wheels and blades.

Just as I thought about getting back into the cab to arm myself with the long thick wooden stick I always kept there I saw the reason for my troubles.

Entwined tightly around the ploughs coulters were a couple of strands of wire, bright silver annoying wires, that it was obvious to me that someone had left discarded half buried in the earth. The earth of *my* field.

With the uneven throbbing of Betsie's neutral engine in my ears and the air around me becoming more and more laden with diesel fumes I rammed the end of my stick betwixt wires and coulter and with biceps straining levered downwards.

I was successful in snapping the stick in two, leaving the wires still taunt and totally embedded in the earth and no closer to freeing up the plough.

I swore into the fading light, threw a freshly pointed stick as far as I could into the field and jumped back into Betsie's cab slamming her into gear as I did so. The old engine struggled to fire and the wheels fought for traction in the mud but slowly I made forward progress expecting any moment to hear the wires at my back ping like guitar strings.

It was then even over the sound of Betsies labouring engine that I heard the shouted voices from somewhere over by the road.

'Whoa, whooaa up, hey stop, you in the tractor, stoppp'

As I turned in my seat to see where the voices were coming from I saw the strangest sight, one that will remain with me for the rest of my life.

What used to be a wire and concrete posted fence running parallel and standing erect along the side of the road was now a domino effect deck of cards laying flat against the ground trying desperately to catch up with me and old Betsie.

Brendan

It hung from the nicotine stained plastic fitting on the ceiling and lying on his back without moving his body he could make it sway backwards and forwards with just his eyes. The single bulb had a blackened area inside it where it had blown a good few weeks ago but he had not got around to replacing it, he just never remembered to.

The back of his head itched because of his damp hair against the makeshift pillow. It felt good when he occasionally scratched at it hard with his long black and bitten nails, he wondered if he could make it bleed, that would stop it itching. And then he was suddenly aware that he was still clutching the broken pool cue in his other hand. Vague memories,

The black ball going into the pocket, the whooping cries of the guys watching and the skinny guy with the sparse ginger hair on his face, snatching up the loose notes from the empty bottle and glass laden table and Pug hitting him hard in the jaw.

Brendan sat up wincing, the metal stays of the bed under him scraped, twisting as he shifted his weight, he sensed the distant wave of pain deep in his head that threatened to visit him later in the day, for now a fugue and the spliff held it at bay.

Pug, his fat stomach bulging over his jeans as he hit the skinny guy sending him flying through the air.

It was good to laugh, good to release the tension in his bladder and feel the warmth spread through his crotch.

It took one swing, just one.

Brendan grinned inanely as what was left of the heavy pool cue swung wildly and struck the light bulb obliterating it, showering the room with a million fragments of brittle glass shards.

'What a shot, see, I can do it too, just one shot'

He lay back, listening to his own laughter and wondered briefly why his jeans felt warm and wet.

He still had it, didn't he?

*

And then the thump on the door, the heavy thump startling Brendan into a new world of pain and awakening.

*

Brendan matched the end bit of the pool cue he was still holding to the one now protruding from Pugs chest as the fat man lay bleeding to death against his bedroom door.

With a bit of good sellotape Brendan was sure he could have the cue looking as neat as it used to and no-one would see the join.

Pop

The push chair had been on an incline so when the young woman's hands were no longer holding on to it, it rolled away onto the grass verge under the weight of its tiny occupant and came to a gentle halt. The child had been asleep until the left arm of its mother landed with a wet thud somewhere close on the concrete of the pavement. A fine spray of blood coloured the little boy's blond hair a strawberry pink and a large flap of his mother's loose warm skin landed like a heavy sodden blanket over his tiny legs. Further thudding sounds came to the infant's ears but by now he had begun to cry, a cry that carried to the people watching, the people standing rooted to the spot unable to take their eyes from the terror unfolding before them.

I too had been watching transfixed from the balcony of my apartment. It had been the first one I had actually seen. I was not actually *'looking'* if you know what I mean but when somebody explodes in front of your very eyes you *see it*, no, you *feel* it. For a good few days now the televised news had been full of it, the front pages of every newspaper taken up with an abundance of horrifying stories and gory photographs. People were exploding, at random, their bodies bursting from the inside out, spewing their innards into the air and sending fragmented limbs in all directions.

'Scientists believe the phenomenon is caused by an airborne virus, scaremongers say it is part of a new wave of chemical warfare delivered by terrorists, some say it is part of an attack from alien life forms, air condition buildings, get into air conditioned buildings, it can't get to you there"

The shouts are coming from all around me. I am running. In amongst a crowd of hysterical stampeding people I am running. The ground below me is slippery with blood and the expelled guts of others.

I try not to look at the riderless motorbike that is crashing into the wall to my left, the woman with the shopping bags screaming as a rain of gore soaks her from head to foot. Another thud, another limb falls in front of me, I skirt around it almost losing my balance.

The air conditioned library is only metres from me, my chest heaves as I run, I feel a popping noise in my ears I run, I feel my face getting warm , I can see the sign for the library but someone's erupted torso hangs over the last four letters in a shredded and bloody shawl ..Lib.. I'm getting nearer, nearer, almost there, my face is getting warmer, my heart is thumping in my chest...I'm almost there, I'm almost…

Helter Skelter

Helter Skelter…'in disorderly haste or confusion'

'I don't think I've ever seen one that tall' Gemma's voice was lost to the sounds of carnival music and the excited screams and laughter of the huge crowds.
Tim wasn't even looking in her direction, instead his eyes were still glued to the dodgems they had just finished riding on. Gemma patted his arm, drew his attention and pointed to the garishly painted and brightly illuminated Helter Skelter standing against the black sky like a spiral stairway climbing up to the stars.
'Sorry, what?' He mouthed, leaning over the glass and bottle cluttered table

between them and cupping an ear towards her mouth.

'I've never seen such a high ..oh never mind' She was fighting a losing battle to make herself heard over the din and decided that she needed another drink. Picking up her empty glass and waving in front of Tim's face and with a grossly exaggerated cough she finally got her boyfriend's full attention.

He stood, smiled and without saying a word took her glass with his own and disappeared into the interior of the bar. Gemma watched him go, he'd be there for a while, the pub was very busy, the funfair was in full swing and a lot of people were out for the evening enjoying themselves.

And the Helter Skelter stood majestically, its tapered walls disappearing into the black of the night sky.

*

'Bar's open till two'

Gemma hadn't noticed Tim's return until she felt the jarring movement of the tired and rickety bench as he sat back down on it; she had been thinking deeply about something, almost asleep, in a trance, staring unblinking at the Helter Skelter and wondering what it would feel like to..

Tim pushed a full glass of frothing lager along the table towards her, 'two o'clock' he repeated taking a gulp of his beer and wiping his lips with the back of his hand..

'Be back soon'

Would be the last words she ever spoke to Tim as she stood and began the short walk to the tiny ground level mouth of the towering Helter Skelter.

'The bar closes at two'

Would be the words Gemma would ever hear from Tim.

*

The scruffy man in the dirty white shirt and waistcoat with long grey hair tied back in a ponytail dismissed her proffered money with a flick of his wrist and handed her a folded piece of thick matting.

'Don't look back' he said and his smile revealed a mouthful of black and decayed teeth.

'Don't you dare look back' *he said again and then he was bending down out of view, no doubt picking out another piece of thick matting for his next potential ..victim.*

Puzzled by the scruffy man's words and her own thoughts Gemma wasted no time in trying to make sense of them, the spiral staircase leading up into the Helter Skelter beckoning and somehow daring her to ascend.

*

When did the carnival's music cease to assail her ears? When did the bright

lights that once filled her eyes dim and become just the dull pewter of a cloud covered moon?'
When did the sensation of being completely alone in the belly of a Helter Skelter that reached up into the sky creep into her soul and cool her blood?
When did she realise that she could not dare to look back no more than she could turn herself on the narrow steps and descend them.

*

'Watch out where yer going yung un, you in a hurry fer yer grave?'
The voice came from somewhere behind her and Gemma had to move quickly to avoid the horse colliding with her back. She jumped sideways and almost lost her footing in the thick mud at her feet and watched as the fully laden cart made its clumsy way past her. The scruffy driver grinned, his mouth full of black and

decaying teeth, his long grey hair tied in a ponytail at his back.

Another voice this time a female's loud and strident and near at her side.

'You determin' to leave me a lone widow aintch yer, yer useless slip of a waif'

Gemma moved the wicker basket from one aching arm to the other and eventually tore her eyes away from the lone oak standing tall in the field, silhouetted black against a darkening sky.

Sometimes when she stared at it she could imagine it as a spiral stairway climbing up to the stars festooned with lights of all colours and people dancing under its spreading limbs.

But mostly she only ever saw just a tree. Just a tree.

It never failed to amaze me

It never failed to amaze me - I always thought of myself as quite a fastidious type of person - you know putting the top back on the toothpaste, ironing my jeans with a careful eye for creases, spreading my sandwiches with cream cheese so that every square millimetre had about the same amount of cheese covering it-then why did all the blood and gristle not bother me? I knew I had to dispose of Sarah "neatly" as it were, but you try sawing up your average twenty-five year old female into sizable bits and not leave too much of a mess.

The arms were not too much trouble - I thought about sawing through the wrist bones first, then I realised that, why do that, when I could take them off at the shoulder and fold them at the elbows-fits nicely into your common or garden Tesco's Supermarket carrier bag. The legs were the same - although more blood escaped from the larger arteries. I decided to saw through the upper thigh and not waste time and effort going back to saw through the thinner part of the ankles just to remove the feet, I was sure that with a little bit of leverage I could break the bones there and maybe would only need to clip off a few toes with my garden shears.

The neck gave me less problems than I had anticipated-although of course she was looking at me the whole time - it did occur to me to remove the eyes, but what's the point of a bit of D.I.Y. when there is nobody to look at your work? I had to change the blade of the little

saw twice during severing the neck as the vertebrae were a bit wet and slippery and it got stuck in the gristle pads between them, also

her long blonde hair was getting in the way constantly. Her head weighed a lot more than I had expected - but then again Sarah was quite an educated young lady a few hours ago.

I remember the next day at work in the tea room my so-called mates reading in the local paper about my handiwork. "What sort of bastard does this to a woman?" someone said - I nearly said, "The type of person who likes cream cheese in their sandwiches" but I didn't. I smiled and carried on with my crossword.

Lady Winsure will see you now

'Lady Winsure will see you now'
The huge black iron gate creaked loudly on its rusted hinges and the butler or

should I say stout man in a stouter suit stood back unmistakingly reluctant to allow me to pass'

I didn't miss the scornful look he gave me as my boots crunched for the first time on the gravel of Lady Winsures private drive. The huge imposing house stood before me in all its majestic glory towering above, proud and haughty. I was overcome by an uncanny sensation that my admittance to it was not and could not be of my own volition.

'This way Dr. Pattison'

The forced whisper of a voice came to me from a small door almost hidden from sight and at the side of the magnificent facade of the main building.

Before approaching the source of the voice I glanced over my shoulder and was surprised to notice that the stout butler was nowhere to be seen.

'Dr. Pattison, Dr. Pattison, the voice came again and this time it sounded slightly anxious. I swapped my leather bag from one hand to the other and taking long strides made my way to the door and the tall female figure standing over its threshold.

'Oh thank you for attending so soon Dr. Pattison, it is so kind of you'

My initial assumption that the woman addressing me from what was obviously a tradesman's entrance could not possibly be the Lady of the house was soon dispelled as she offered a white lace gloved hand for me to take in mine. Her elegant attire was immaculate and her tone of voice cultured and refined.

'I can not tell you how relieved I am to make your acquaintance in such dire circumstances'.

I couldn't help but notice that all the while the Lady spoke to me she made no eye contact with me but quick and furtive glances over my shoulder.

'Come, this way'

Her hand was on my shoulder and before I could take stock of what was happening I was ushered into the shadows of the huge building with a surprising amount of urgency.

'Its Melissa, you see, she's not well, not well at all'

*

Empty does not describe it in any way, better, devoid of anything. The large dark foyer I found myself in had me in mind of an abandoned property, one that had not seen a living soul in a good few years. It had a cold damp lingering in its sombre walls and an absolute silence that was more fitting to a cemetery.

'This way, Dr. Pattison, please do not dally, I fear Melissa is not at all well'

And in a blur of lace and sequins the Lady Winsure was headed for the broad and highly polished wooden staircase that dominated the whole scene.

And it was then that I realised I hadn't, as yet, uttered a single word.

*

We finally reached the voluminous landing after a rapid ascension of the stairs and I was astounded to notice that the long oak panelled corridors were illuminated by mounted conche shaped lamps that for all the world appeared as if they were fueled by gas.

But I had no time to loiter, Lady Winsure was disappearing into the flickering shadows like a rabbit down a warren.

And then at one of the many doors that led off from the corridor she stopped and turned to face me as, out I breath, I caught up with her.

'Melissa's room, but I beg your forgiveness I can not bring myself to enter it again'

Her eyes pleaded with mine as she spoke and I took it from her stance that I was expected to enter the room alone. I placed a hand on the cold brass doorknob and with a little effort turned it clockwise, opened the door and entered.

*

The room was in semi-darkness, the only light being a narrow wedge of sunlight squeezing through a gap in heavy velvet drapes at the tall sash windows.

I had only taken two steps into it when I heard the door at my back click closed and heard footsteps disappearing down the corridor the same way I had come.

I was a G.P. of over 25 years standing and my inbred instincts were to seek out my potential patient and ignore all else so I was immediately drawn to the unmoving shape under the heavy blankets of the four poster bed. Something was wrong, something terribly wrong.

We were in what I would assume was the building's main room, high ceilinged and draughty. Large canvas covered shapes told me that the furniture had been covered in readiness for being moved, to where was not my concern or indeed my interest, my thoughts now were in Lady Winsure and my call of duty.

*

'It does no harm, we all leave well alone'
We were standing at the large sash windows staring out at the vastly overgrown gardens.
William, the man I assumed to be Lady Winsure's butler, held my gaze as he spoke.

'It's been fourteen years, she is not going to change now, I wish I had not done what I did but I can not undo it now'

I saw a tear forming in his eye and he lowered his face to look at the worn wooden floorboards beneath our feet.

And then he raised his head to look me once again in the eye.

It was her idea to call the china doll I gave her Melissa after my young niece died all those years ago not mine.

The Movies

'Yes, Mrs Mitchel we will get unloading as soon as we've had a bit of a break'

'Well I would like it done before it gets too dark'

'Mrs Mitchel we have just driven almost 120 miles, a thirty minute break isn't going to make us much later'

'Well please make sure it is only thirty minutes, I haven't paid your company for you to keep taking breaks, we were at that service area for almost an hour'

'Don't worry Mrs. Mitchel we will have you unloaded in no time'

Danny had the lorry's window fully down and could hear every word, he was smiling to himself as he heard Mick walk round to the drivers door and wrench it open.

'Fucking frigid old bag'

Mick's timing was spot on, the noise of the slamming of the cab's door drowned out both his shouted profanities and Danny's guffaws.

'Now, now he managed to say between gulps of breath, 'The customers always right'

'Fuck the customer' Mick responded reaching over lorry's considerable dashboard for his crumpled packet of cigarettes.

'I suppose a cup of tea and salmon sandwiches with the crust cut off is out of the question'

Danny was hoping his quip would lighten the mood but he suddenly became painfully aware of who the removal company had lumbered him with for today's move.

Mick fucking Morrison.

*

'No mention of a Mr. Mitchel'

Danny had finished his mars bar and flicked the empty wrapper out of the cab's wide open window he glanced around just in time to see Mick's hand go for the door handle.

'He's either fucked of with the barmaid or that old bag has killed 'im'

Danny couldn't suppress a giggle, he pulled on his heavy duty gloves and followed Mick out of the cab and around to the back of the removal truck.

'My old lady always said I'd be in the movie business'

Danny feigned a laugh, Mick always came out with that old one and he didn't want to upset him by ignoring his overworked joke, having to work with Mick was bad enough.

She was standing in the doorway, her arms crossed over her ample bosom, she made a big show of staring at the tiny gold watch on her wrist.

Her mouth was working but neither Mick or Danny heard a word she was saying.

'Lets, get this load out of here and get back before the fucking pubs shut'

They had the lorry's back doors open and Mick was staring at the few boxes and furniture scattered about in its cavernous interior.

Danny repeated what he had said when they were loading up the removal lorry a good few hours ago.

'The old girl aint got much in the way of furniture, this job shouldn't take too long'

*

And it didn't take too long.

With only a few bits and pieces left to unload Danny thought he sense of change in the old ladies demeanour so he took a chance.

'Don't suppose there's any chance of a cuppa, is there Misses, we've nearly finished 'ere?'

Mrs Mitchel's sigh was seismic but Danny was happy to see her turn away and make for the kitchen.

*

On the tray resting on one of the last wooden crates still sitting on the gravel was a china teapot, two cups, a bowl of sugar and a jug of milk. Mick grinned widely over it at Danny and for a brief second Danny thought he was actually beginning to loathe him a little less.

*

'It's beginning to get dark'

Mrs.Mitchel had appeared out on the gravel drive as if from nowhere, she picked up the used tray and took it back to the house.

'It's beginning to get closer to closing time' Mick said to Danny.

*

'That one needs to go up into the main bedroom'

Mrs Mitchel was pointing at one of the last crates.

'Yeah, the fucking heaviest Mick said under his breath.

Danny already had a grip of one end of it, Mick wiped his nose on his sleeve and got hold of the other.

*

It happened halfway up the stairs, Mick's fingers slipped from under the crate and with a sickening thud it crashed down onto the stairs. The force of the blow splintered its base and Mr Mitchel unceremoniously fell out and rolled, bumping down each stair trailing a stream of blood in his wake.

Mrs Mitchel screamed hysterically at Mick through her hands covering her mouth.

'How the hell am I going to get the blood out of that beautiful carpet ?'

Rick's Room

It was four floors up and through a window layered with thick grease and grime you could just make out the arguing railway lines and the 4.30pm train from Reading, assuming of course you were peering out of it just as the 4.30pm from Reading was due in at

Paddington at the precise time you were looking.

'Is he going to write like that all the way through this book?'

I hear you say.

'Yes' so if you don't like it, put the book back in the charity shop where you found it and forget it…and me (my name's Rick and I'm 19 years old).

*

It didn't matter about the lack of running water. Rick used the free facilities in the station or if he got caught short for a wee he could pull up the sash window a little bit and relieve himself onto Eastbourne Terrace enough floors below.

A bare flex hung uselessly in the middle of the ceiling, there was no longer an electric supply to feed it and the plaster which barely held it in or covered the dead wires was cracked and crumbling.

Who needed electricity when candles and paraffin for a heater were so cheap? The walls which were once probably painted an off white were now a lot more off white and tinged with dull shades of nicotine yellow and other far more unpleasant substances. In one wall was a narrow door that opened into a coffin shaped cupboard, its interior heavily shrouded with cobwebs and giving off a cloying odour of decay. Rick closed the door and was happy to see a latch to secure it.

On the floor and sticking in places to the bare floorboards a rat bitten edged threadbare carpet lay moist, mouldy and moving with insects giving off an odour which mingled with the foetid smell already in attendance proclaiming this domain as extremely unhealthy.

Oh, I forgot to mention the ravaged curtains, although the steam engines had ceased running almost ten years ago they were black with soot and heavy with dried oil grease stains and long dead insect remains.

The skeletal body of a crow hung upside down from the guttering above the window but Rick hadn't got around to dislodging it yet, after all it wasn't doing him any harm.

But the best part of all this was the fact that Rick didn't have to pay any rent. The entire building was derelict and totally forgotten, hidden in a maze of back streets and secluded alleys that were only frequented by foxes, rats and a few more like ricks.

The bullying bastard that mum chose over Rick could rot in hell.

*

Apart from all this Rick was protective of his little flat and after a hard day's work at the local council landfill and a pint or two, a pork pie or cheese and onion sandwich (cockles if the cockleman showed up) at the Victoria Inn Rick was ready to climb into his sleeping bag on the floor of the empty building and shiver himself to sleep.

That was of course until he met Adrian.

*

'They said they weren't taking anyone else on?'

It was the new bloke's (not shitted up yet) yellow hi vis that first caught Rick's eye. He wasn't one of the gaffers, too young looking and scrawny and the three old men were working a good distance away. Dragging his spade through the thick layer of rubbish strewn alongside the ground at the edges of the mountainous mound of household waste Rick closed the gap between himself and the *new bloke*.

The *new bloke* seemed to be ignoring him, he was staring in the other direction at the cloud of scavenging seagulls squabbling over bits of carrion rotting in the hot sun.

'Stinks, dun it?'

The *'new bloke'* spoke but he didn't move.

Rick drew up alongside him, hefting his dirty bladed shovel onto his shoulder with one hand and pushing his tangled greasy hair out of his eyes with the other.

'You get used to it' he said, kicking up a storm of dust at his feet with toe capped boots and spitting a wodge of thick green phlegm from the side of his mouth.

*

'What's yer name?'

They were in the temporary prefab hut that smelt of urine and tobacco drinking overly mashed tea from heavily stained china mugs.

The three older men sitting at a table and smoking stinking roll ups totally ignoring *'the kids'*

'Adrian, but call me Aidie, I fucking hate Adrian'

'You look like an Adrian'

Rick thought, but kept it to himself.

'You can't sit there all day holding hands' It was one of the older men, chairs scraping along the floor as they got up and made their way laughing to the prefab's only door.

'We got ourselves a couple of fairies' another one said and the laughter carried on until the three men were walking back towards the awaiting festering mounds.

'Fuck them' Adrian said, putting his used cup in a large stained, stainless steel sink.

*

Adrian took the small sealed brown envelope from the tall man wearing the ill-fitting suit jacket and without opening put it in the pocket of his faded donkey jacket.

The first thing Rick did when he received *his* wages was open the envelope and count its contents.

Maybe Rick should help the scrawny 'new bloke' called Adrian count *his* wages.

*

A couple of times Rick was forced to step sideways into a shop doorway or into a deserted alleyway. A couple of times Rick was sure he had been seen.

Adrian walked fast, Rick had a job to keep up with him, but it was late and getting dark, Rick had nothing else to do and besides it was fun, he'd catch up with him soon and he had a great idea.

He'd take him back and show him his little fourth floor room.

*

The man with the ill fitting jacket handed Rick a small sealed brown envelope.

'What happened to your scrawny little mate? He hasn't been back since last pay day?'

'Dunno' replied Rick and he was not my mate'

Rick turned away just as the man spoke again.

'Oh, by the way, some woman asked to give you this'

He handed Rick a folded piece of note paper.

*

Rick read the note over and over again. And then he finally went home, the bastard was gone.

*

The police were called and then forensics. The demolition workers had complained about the smell coming from a secured cupboard in one of the fourth floor rooms..

It was the body of a young man, he had been tied up with wire and gagged with a leather thong.

They said he'd probably been dead for about two weeks.

In the pocket of his donkey jacket they found a pay packet.

Unopened.

No cause for alarm

I've been dead now for almost seven years. It takes a while being dead before you begin to learn all the nuances about actually being dead. Ask any dead person, they'll tell you,(oh, I just realised, you can't, can you?).

My memories of being alive are disjointed and not the least bit in any chronological order. Recollections overlap and become vague and remote, like early morning dreams if you fall asleep again, so real whilst in your mind but turning to dust when you try to grasp them, to hold onto them.

Here's the thing, faces. No matter how hard you try you cannot remember faces or even picture them.

Maybe a name or two will appear from out of the twilight of your mind once and again but you have no faces to put to the names.

Being dead I think is meant to be like that.

Merciful.

This is what makes my recent little *jaunt* (I use that word because it is the only one that springs to mind) so beguiling, so *out there.*

*

Being dead for the amount of time I have has bestowed upon me certain privileges.

One of which is to visit places that in life meant something to me albeit fleetingly. Strictly places not people.
My old school.

*

A wide flight of stairs, echoing the footsteps of a thousand hurrying schoolchildren no longer hurrying anywhere.
Double doors, glass and wooden, no longer a barrier for the likes of me.
The library, expansive and book infested. I'd spent many an hour here/there engrossed in the written word. My seat by the window, my reading occasionally interrupted by sights of the antics of my school friends on the playground two floors below.
I can afford to sit here for a moment or two.
Despite the alarm.

*

'Ok Dave, seems like another false alarm, let's just get the checks done on the rest of the building, and reset everything and we're done here'
'Wait a minute Pete, there is someone in there, the library, someone is sitting by the window….look'
'Where?'
'Nah, must be a trick of the light, I can't see anybody, I think you're overworked mate, I think you're seeing ghosts'

Over the garden fence

'Yep, I finally did it, I finally got rid of the old sod'
The rough texture on the top of the wooden trellis was digging into Agne's fleshy forearm but listening to Hilda's rants was always worth it. Besides, it was a good half an hour before Corry.

'You won't hear him singing 'Don't go under the apple tree with anyone else but me' at two o'clock in the bloody morning anymore'

'Oh, Hilda, you are so funny'

'Well, I ask you didn't that get on your bloody nerves, every Saturday night from the pub?'

'I must admit…'

'It wouldn't have been so bad if he had changed his tune once in a while'

'He did overdo it..'

'Ow about, On Mothers Kelly's doorstep, or Get me to the Church on time'

'He did make a bit of a din, woke my 'arold up once and he sleeps like..'

'I threw a bucket of water over him once'

'No, did you really?'

'Freezing cold it was'

'Did that stop..'

'Nah he just burst into 'Raindrops keep falling on my head'

'Oh, my Hilda, you do make me laugh, anyway how on earth did you get rid of the old sod like you said?'

'I slit his throat with a Wilco bread knife as he was asleep last night'

Vacuum

His name was Pele and we all loved him, he was a bright yellow budgerigar (not a canary) and in the evenings Pele would be let out of his cage (with all of the room's windows closed) to fly freely around and land on our heads.

Dad was at work, my sisters were playing hopscotch out the front on the pavement and my brother was out helping the milkman on his rounds.

The house was quiet until…

I could hear mum screaming from the back garden where I was digging up worms to go fishing. I ran into the front room to be greeted with the sight of mum standing rigid by Pele's open cage, holding the vacuum cleaner nozzle in one hand and the other tightly clamped to her mouth, stifling what without a doubt was further hysterical screams.

As I approached she took the hand from her mouth and made pointing gestures with her index finger between the open door of Pele's cage and the tiny black mouth of the vacuum cleaner hose.

I looked at one to the other and then I noticed the small yellow feathers drifting on the air from the breeze coming in from the back door and bigger feathers stuck to wires of the cage's open door.

I went rigid on the spot as it slowly dawned me what mum had just done.

A vision of Pele frantically flapping his wings with all his might against the immense suction power of the Electrolux Z345 was imprinted in my brain along with my mum's (it wasn't my fault) look in her terrified eyes.

I lowered myself to my knees snatching at the dual catches on each side of the vacuum cleaner that was now almost certainly the unwitting instrument of poor old Pele's gruesome demise.

With the back cover of the machine removed I held my breath realising that my eyes had been shut tight against the horrible sight that was about to greet me and then due to overwhelming morbid curiosity I opened them.

Pele was beakfirst flat against the Electrolux Z345's dust filter doing a brilliant impersonation of a spread eagle as if viewed from the back.

My mum was shouting in my ear 'Is he alive, is he alive ? Oh my God I've killed him, I was only doing what I always do, hovering all the muck of the bottom of his cage and then 'Phloop' Pele was gone'

I prised Pele off the filter and he immediately flew from my hand to his favourite perching place on top of the curtain pelmets.

Pele had survived the hoovering and lived for quite a time after and the featherless bald patch on the top of his head looked quite fetching after a while. Mum never used the Electrolux Z345 to clean his cage again.

Four Days

It was one of those smiles that tells you that the smiler is sharing a joke with you. A joke between just you and him. No, on second thoughts maybe 'joke' is the wrong word. Secret. Maybe secret is a better word. A secret between just you and him. Again I struggled to find the right word or way to describe the smile I saw on his face, a smile that had no right to turn into a laugh.

Day One

06.30 the flatbed is loaded up, the sun is peeking over the rooftops and three spent cigarette butts flicked away into the gutter, Big Dave didn't like you smoking in the cab of his flatbed.
The radio drowned out the familiar sounds of tubes, couplers, mast climbers, planks and

various other scaffold paraphernalia loseley laid behind the cab and loud boisterous chatter drowned out the sound of the radio.

The job was two miles out of town, planned for 7 days and we could easily do it in 4 if we cut to the chase.

It would be all ready for the builders to use for whatever they wanted it erected for and when they'd finished we would take it all down. Big Dave was already on the case.

'Let's get the gear unloaded, sorted against the wall and prepared before we even think of tea'

I grabbed a couple of poles, Andy an armful of couplers and we laid them out neatly on the concrete pathway, Big Dave was busy placing the pedestrian walkway warnings and all the other 'take care' signs necessary for working on the facade of a three storey building.

The sun was coming up, the pretty young mothers smiled as they walked children to school and Big Dave seemed to be in a buoyant mood.

Day Two

'Yep, she's pregnant'

'Great news Dave, congratulations' Andy and I said almost in unison.

'First one Dave?'

Andy said, trying to sound remotely interested and giving me a sly wink over Big Dave's shoulder.

'Yep' Big Dave said, stepping down from the cab of the flatbed.

'First one'

Andy and I lit up a smoke each and leant across the body of the flatbed, Big Dave wasn't going to push us too much today that was for sure.

*

We'd connected all the adjustable legs, attached the horizontal braces, increased the height of the tower and were well on the way to attaching the second platform, things were going well.

When Big Dave suggested having a quick pint after work to celebrate the growing foetus who were we to refuse?

Day Three

Big Dave was in his usual shitty mood, it was becoming blatantly obvious that having a baby now came second place to getting the scaffolding up and ready.
Andy and I were still laughing about the fact that Big Dave had said a pint and *a pint* was exactly what he meant. When he left the pub we had five more.
The day was hot which didn't make our hangovers feel any better. We could have finished the job if we really pushed ourselves but we still had the fourth day to go so we didn't.
Big Dave did nothing but moan under his breath and occasionally wander off which suited us fine.
Tomorrow we would secure all access to the scaffold, attach the guardrails and inspect our work for safety, job done.

Day Four.

'We'll be finished by mid-day' Andy said, taking a last big drag from his cigarette and flicking it out 60 ft to the ground below.

We were sitting on the top flatform enjoying the warming sun, looking over the rooftops at the surrounding buildings. Big Dave was nowhere in sight.

'Where is Big Dave anyway?' Andy was standing up, his knees cracking and the scaffold planks gently settling under the movement of his weight.

'I've no idea' I replied 'Last time I saw him he was checking all the guardrails'

Andy took another cigarette from his packet and offered one to me.

Neither of us felt the slight movement on the boards below us. We were used to them shifting when a heavy vehicle like a double decker bus passed by.

Andy was grinning at me and before I could speak he was talking again.

'I had a weird dream last night'

'Big Dave was giving his missus one' can you imagine that what a horrible thought? 'Like two beached whales rutting between two fucking great big sandunes'

I couldn't help but picture it and grin.

Andy hadn't finished, he raised his voice over the passing traffic..

'As I watched them the beach shook and the sanddunes began to collapse, just like a fucking earthquake.

Well that was it, I was holding my belly in fits of laughter.

'And then a big tsunami sprang up and hurtled towards this ship way out in the…

Andy leant away from me and put a hand out to the guardrail that wasn't there...and I saw his face as he began his plummet of 60ft to the solid concrete below..and he was smiling..

It was one of those smiles that tells you that the smiler is sharing a joke with you. A joke between just you and him. No, on second thoughts maybe 'joke' is the wrong word. Secret. Maybe secret is a better word. A secret between just you and him. Again I struggled to find the right word or way to describe the smile

I saw on his face, a smile that had no right to turn into a screaming laugh.

Not a lot to say

Forgive me dear reader if I lapse periodically into an unexplained silence but

        see it just happened then. I can't help myself.

    many years ago I was unfortunate enough to witness and experience such an unaccountable occasion that it rendered me speechless

   not in the sense that I was totally lost for words but in a way that speaking or writing continuously is something I am no longer capable of.

   you may find it a source of irritation but I beg that you persevere, tolerate my accursed affliction and avail yourself of my disturbing recollections.

it was a pleasant enough day

the
sun was going down and the shadows
darkening when our teacher, Mr Adams
suggested that we ceased our working outdoor
and

make our way back into the
classroom bringing our various efforts of
artwork with us.
I was particularly proud
of my
work and as such compelled to finish my
painting of the huge statue standing proud in
the schoolyards garden whilst

the dwindling light still favoured me.

that
was until I heard Mr Adams raised voice at the
classroom's open window and realised I was
the only pupil still outside.

lets have you back inside.

and of
course now he was addressing me personally.
 with a flamboyant flourish I gathered my
painting under one arm and with an equally
flamboyant but infantile flourish I waved
goodby to the huge statue, the very object that
had held my undivided attention for the whole

of that unforgettable afternoon
it waved back

i was rendered speechless.

A Long Road Ahead

I have been watching them for quite a while
now. From my position high up on this grassy
hill I have had a constant view and I have
been privy to many changes.
There are a few huddles of bushes and shrubs
here and there but they do not pose any
problems regarding my observations because
they are on a far lower level than myself.

The land below me dips gently into a wide valley, carved out of the rock thousands of years ago by what was then a raging river.
Of course that was long before my time and all of this I have gleaned from the words of the winds and the inherent knowledge gained from the unstoppable passage of time.
What remains of the raging river has narrowed, slowed and it is now no more than a meandering stream.
As early as I can remember the people started constructing arches across this water and mud lanes to connect with wider mud lanes until the lanes became solid in appearance eventually merging, one with the other.
But these recently arrived people are different, frighteningly different, with their huge wheeled, cloud belching animals and heaps of sand and blocks of square cut stones.
I watch as they toil through all weathers, sun, rain and snow during the hours of daylight and also through the hours of darkness, totally unperturbed.
I watch from my hill as the sun goes down and I am amazed that the strange people make

their own light so that they can move it to any place they require. Sometimes the glow from the light that emanates from them turns the sky above and on the horizon an unnatural shimmering orange.

Under my unremitting gaze they work like fevered ants constructing a solid grey, wide lane greatly surpassing all others.

*

I often wonder what other occurrences, if any, awaits me and the duration of time that needs to elapse between each occasion.

Since the year 1678 and the raging Pendle witch that spitefully laid her black curse on me, I have neither suffered for, nor regretted my long life.

May it continue on for many years to come. Albeit as a tree.

Part Time

Sometimes I can get my letters out without having to unlock the little door. If I can reach them by squeezing my fingers

into the narrow slot I can tease them out.
Today I couldn't, the postman had
pushed them too far in.
I used my key. My name is Neville.
The man in the beard was standing
behind me. I heard his tut tutting and
could smell the smell of old he always
wore like a coat.
And then he was talking to someone, me.
'Bills, that's all I get nowadays'
I answered with a nod and words that I
didn't really want to speak.
'I always do as well'.
His little letter door has the number 5 on
it, I'm glad mine doesn't have the number
6 or 4.
Somebody is having bacon for breakfast.
I go up the stairs to my room on the
second floor and leave the man in the
beard where he is.

*

He even looks like a boss. His eyes are too blue and the wrinkles around them are tight and deep. He wears a suit and highly polished shoes. I can tell he has a wife because he always smells of soap. He speaks to me as if I'm 10 years old. I'm used to it now.

'Gonna be busy today, gonna be hectic Neville'

He likes that word 'hectic' ; everything for him is 'hectic' if it isn't, he wants it to be. He gives me the key to the store room, most of the boxes that were delivered yesterday will be where I left them.

I put on the brown coat with the big side pockets and reach into the right hand side one for the knife he gave me almost a year ago. Bright red plastic with a retractable blade.

I hear his voice from the front of the store.

'Get a move on, it's gonna be hectic today'.

A year ago…

'You'll like him Neville he is a nice man' Mum had my jacket in her hand, she handed it to me.
'Don't be late and talk up, no mumbling, only stupid people mumble'

*

"We are relocating Sue, there is no way I can keep him on even if I wanted to'
She was sitting up in the bed, she wouldn't cover herself up yet, sometimes he would surprise her.
'You can't just dismiss him Gary, you know what Neville is like he'd never get another job the way he is'
'I've put up with him for over a year, I only took him on for a favour to you, he'll have to find something else'

And then he slid his hand over to cup a breast and surprised her.

*

The man in the beard was standing on the landing talking to the lady with the stick, they saw me and stopped talking together, instead he talked to me.
'You off to work?'
She looked at her stick and said nothing.
I said yes.
Because I was.

*

Even she was acting strange, the woman in the office on the typewriter, Kate, she watched me as I walked into the storeroom but looked away quickly when I looked at her.
I could smell the soap getting closer and then he was behind me, close.
'I've got to let you go Neville, I'll give you a weeks notice but I've got to let you go'

*

I didn't start crying until I was alone at lunchtime sitting on a box looking at the sandwiches I bought where I always bought them from the stall on the station platform. I didn't want anybody to see me crying, a grown man.

If the man in the beard was standing in my way on the stairs again I was going to push him out of the way.

He wasn't.

*

I'd got the one and only letter out of my box by squeezing my fingers into the slot, I didn't need to get my key out.

…sorry but you can't come back here

….I'm sure you can find another job somewhere and besides it's such a lovely flat we found for you…be sure to sign on…

Love Mum. x

I don't remember seeing any of the other words in the letter.

How did mum know that the boss had *let me go?*

*

Strange kind of pretty, glasses hanging around her neck on a thin cord of what looked like leather. I tried not to look at her too often but my eyes kept going where I tried to stop them going. The name on her badge was Laura, I didn't want her to see me too often, to get used to seeing me, she'd know I wasn't just reading.

The library was warmly quiet and nobody knew me, knew who I and the boss had *let me go..* I pretended to read books and looked occasionally at the lady with the glasses, Laura.

The mornings went quickly but the afternoons dragged on until it was late enough for me to go back to the flat.

Dinner time I'd go to a cafe and have tea and chips.

The men came in and made a lot of noise, scrapping chairs and laughing and talking. I tried to not notice but they took me in with them with their eyes.

'You wanna make some quick money lad?'

He was leaning over me and smelt like wooden fences.

'A days graft and thirty quid no questions asked'

I said ok.

He slapped me on the back and walked back to the table where the other men were eating and talking.

I looked over at them as many times as I dared, making my cold chips last as long as I could.

When one of them stood up and walked to the counter I thought they had forgotten all about me.

'Tomorrow, here, 8.o'clock'
And then they were gone.

*

The man in the beard stood aside as I
made my way up the stairs to my flat. He
didn't say anything, he didn't know the
boss had *let me go,* I certainly wasn't
going to tell him.
I watched the t.v. thought about ringing
mum, ..*sorry but you can't come back
here..be sure to sign on..*
I'll have breakfast in the cafe at 08.00
tomorrow, while I wait for the men.
Is that all the man in the beard does,
stand on the stairs and wait for me?

*

Two of them, '*lads*' eating toast looking
over at me all the time and pretending not
to. The one with the ginger hair spoke
'You waiting for them as well bud?'
'Yes'

It was 08.25 I almost got up and left but the other two 'lads' were still sitting, talking, so I made my cold tea last longer. The men came in at 08.45 they didn't order anything they just looked at all three of us and said 'Fit?'

*

The van was cramped and rusty, it smelt of petrol and chips. It hit every bump on the narrow country lane and screeched when we parked outside a huge house at the end of a long tree lined drive.

The men lit cigarettes and left the three of us in our seats looking out of the dirty windows wondering about the £30.

'What's your name?'

He was sitting in front of me between the other two looking over his shoulder at me.

'Neville'

'What sort of a fucking name is Neville'

The two either side of him laughed with
him
'Fucking Neville they said
And laughed again. I'd heard it all before
it was nothing new.

*

The men were back, sliding the door of
the van open.
It was cold outside. I wished I was back
in the cafe.
But £30.

*

A large flat back vehicle pulled up just
ahead of the smell of hot pitch, its back a
cloud of rising smoke and black molten
tar.
The men gave us shovels, we used them
to spread the hot molten tar over the
drive and flattened it down.

*

Just before the mound of unloaded tar
was spread the flatbed left to get another

load. The men got in the van and left us to wait.

That was when Nick, Barry and Mike leaned on their shovels, lit cigarettes and turned their attention to me.

'Hey, Neville, are you into girl's mate ?' Nick was the one who spoke and the others laughed every time he did.

I told them of course I was.

We worked until the flat bed was once again clear of tar and was driven away.

The men gave us crumpled up notes and told us to be in the cafe the next morning. We went back to the cafe in the van with aching arms listening to the loud radio and the men talking and loudly laughing.

*

Max watched him from the driver's seat of the van, he watched him for most of the day, the one they called Neville. He watched as Neville did twice as much work as the other lazy bastards, he watched as the others leaned on their shovels and laughed and smoked. Max watched and made up his mind.

*

'Does 'ee ever speak to you?'
The man in the beard was leaning against the stair post looking down the stairs at the skinny girl with the baby at number 3.
'Says hello, good morning sometimes'
'I think 'ees, you know, gay'
'Never see 'im with a lass, but then I never seen 'im with a bloke, come to think of it I ain't never seen 'im with nobody'
The baby started to cry again.
'Fuck it' the skinny girl said pushing the front door open with her bony elbow and disappearing out into the street.

2

'When did you last work? What date?
Have you got your P.45? Fill in this form
and bring or send it back to me'
I didn't tell her I was getting money from
Max for laying tar, somewhere different
every other day.
Sometimes the van was full of rubbish
and we took it off into the woods and just
left it in the bushes. As I say I didn't tell
her anything. Max told me not to. Max
was a big man with big muscles and I
knew you did what Max told you to do.
I didn't have to work with Nick, Barry and
Mick anymore, Max told me he had told
them all to 'fuck off' they were lazy
bastards. They didn't argue.

*

'Have you heard anything from Neville
since…?'
Gary was slipping his shirt from his
shoulders.

'Leave well alone' said Sue as she slipped her arms around his naked torso.

'Greenways looking for you'
It was the man in the beard standing in his usual place on the landing.
I heard footsteps coming from the stairs above.
'That time of the month again Mr.Neville'
He always called me Mr.Neville.
He followed me into the flat but stayed in the living room as I went into the bedroom.
'It'll have to go up soon, times ain't getting any easier'
I heard his voice as I bent down to get the box from under the bed.
I gave him the crumpled notes and watched him unfold them and count them.
'Only just right' he said.

He always said that *'Only just right'.* He thought it was funny.
I wondered if he could feel or smell the tar on the notes.

*

'Get that down yer neck'
Max placed the pint glass on the table and slapped me hard on the back.
It was beer and the froth spilt onto the table.
It was a hot day and we both smelt of the tar we'd just laid on a big drive' The pub was in the middle of the big City and busy.
'You've earned it today'
Max swallowed half of his and wiped his mouth with the back of his hand.
The men on the pool table were laughing, staring.
'One of them said something towards Max.
I didn't know they knew him.

Max got up so quick he knocked the table and my glass of beer flew off onto the floor.

He swung his fist and hit the man holding the pool cue hard in his face and his nose went red with blood.

The other man turned away, he looked very frightened.

Max hit the man again and there was blood on the man's face.

Max grabbed the man's hair and pulled his face towards his mouth.

They were on the floor.

Max was biting him and tearing chunks of skin off his face.

Other men had come into the room and they were rushing about swearing and screaming.

Max was laying on the man spitting bits of red meat onto the carpet.

The men held onto Max's legs and tried to drag him off.

Max was barking and yelping like a dog.
I peed myself and stood up, someone
pushed me out of the door into a carpark.
I ran.

*

I went to the cafe the next day and the
next but Max wasn't there.
On the third day he was. He had bruises
all over his face.
'Gotta big job today, you fit ? he said and
slapped me hard on the back.
'Just you and me Nev, never mind the
others, from now on me and you'
He called me Nev.

3

If I kept the curtains open I didn't need to
have any lights on; the light from the
street's lamp posts were just enough to
see by. The T.V. was on but I wasn't

watching it at least I don't remember watching it.

When the knock on the door came it was a moment before I realised the sound was a knock on the door. My door.

'Neville ?' Mum's voice came to me from the landing.

I opened the door.

She stood on the bare wood peering into the room at the silent T.V.

'Why is it so dark in here?'

'And who is he?'

Max reached for his cigarettes and smiled a big smile at Mum.

To have and to…

According to the seating arrangements printed on little cards with gold lettering we were placed with two couples, Tim and Amanda and James and Ruth.

'I wish they wouldn't mix us up like this' Jane said 'I would much rather choose who we sat with'

"I know, same here," I replied, although looking around at a sea of strange faces I could only pick out one or two I vaguely recognized.

'Oh well, I said, 'Let's make the most of it, who knows Tim, Amanda, James and Ruby might be fun to know when we do get to know them'

'Ruth', corrected Jane, 'Ruth not Ruby'

'Ruth' I reiterated.

Where had I seen them before, Tim and Amanda? A long time ago but I'm sure I've seen them before'

*

'Hello, I'm James this is Ruth'

'Hello, I'm Tim, 'this is Amanda'

'Hi I'm David this is Jane' as I spoke I tried to catch Tim's eye, if we did ever meet he showed no sign of remembering me.

Clumsy introductions carried out succinctly and forced smiles exchanged between us.

After which we had only sat down a second before loud applause filled the hall and the newly weds made their way to the centre table with all eyes upon them.

The speeches were echoes of a thousand speeches at a thousand weddings and each one followed by over-exuberant clapping and in some cases back slapping and pecks on the cheek.

And then the unmistakable sound of clanging cutlery accompanied by the smell of hot food filled the air and settled over the masses inducing a babble of uncomfortable smalltalk.

*

It seemed right from the start that Amanda must have thought of herself as a bit of an alpha female picking up the already opened bottle of sparkling wine on the table and offering it around.

'Don't they make a lovely couple ?' she said as she tilted the bottle over Jane's empty glass.

'They do, don't they' my wife responded, lifting her glass from the table and placing it directly below the bottle's neck ensuring any accidental spillage of the contents would be far less likely.

'They look just like Damien and Lucinda don't they Tim?'

It was more than obvious that no-one around the table apart from Tim and Amanda knew who Damien and Lucinda were and the remark was dismissed immediately by all.

'So where do you guys hail from, do I detect an American accent?'

It was James who up until this point had said very little, maybe the wine had emboldened him.

'Fremont, Nebraska'

Tim and Amanda replied almost in unison and the wide grin that passed between them was impossible to miss.

'They certainly do make a lovely couple'

Amanda was topping up Tim's glass and I swear I saw her wink over the top of the bottle at him and then she was addressing all four of us.

'We love weddings, don't you? We go to lots, don't we Tim, if there's a wedding, no matter we go to it, don't we Tim?'

Jane leaned in close to my ear, her words whispered and guarded. *'What a strange thing to say?'*

And then Tim was endorsing what Amanda had just uttered.

'If there's a wedding, we go to it and they do make such a lovely couple'

*

'How do you know the couple, are you related in any way?'
It was obvious Ruth was addressing Jane and myself. She was leaning forward over the busy table and trying to make her voice heard over the noise but it was Amanda who responded first.
'Known 'em for years, haven't we Tim ?
'Years' replied Tim.
And that's when the music started.

*

'Many congratulations Abigail and Matt and you look absolutely beautiful Abigail'
We had left our small table and made our way through dancing couples to the much larger top table and Jane had her hands on the new bride's white laced shoulders.
'Thank you, Auntie Jane, uncle David, it's so good to see you both here'
Abigail smiled at me and Matt winked a manly wink and an uncomfortable pause

ensued and then as far as I was concerned it was job done and thank god Abigail had remembered our names.

*

'They make a lovely couple, don't they?' Amanda said to us when after another battle through the dancing crowds we had finally made our way back to our table.

'Oh, where are James and Ruby?' I asked.

'Ruth' said Jane.

'Gone' said Tim.

'Something about babysitters' said Amanda.

*

I waited patiently for Status Quo to finish 'rocking all over the world' and was rewarded with a slow one to follow. For some strange reason it was good to get away from Tim and Amanda's company and on to the dancefloor with Jane.

Tim and Amanda sat and watched us avidly exchanging grins all the while.

'We make a lovely couple don't we?' Jane whispered in my ear as I held her close. It was good to laugh.

*

The mini bar was the first thing I saw when we finally made it up to our hotel room.

'We did stay a respectable time didn't we David?'

'Of course we did darling' I had two small glasses out on the glass topped table and two smaller plastic bottles of white wine unscrewed and ready.

'We got to say proper goodbyes to Abigail and Matt and I'm sure they would have remembered our names again if it hadn't been for all the booze it was obvious they had imbibed.

'Besides I couldn't stand another minute with that Amanda and Tim..weird bastards weren't they, nothing you could put your finger on but I'm sure I've seen them before.

That's when I got my phone out, a black and white blurred photo from an old newspaper now vivid in my mind.

Google.

Timothy and Amanda Jackson.

Fremont, Nebraska, U.S.A.

Wanted for questioning over the homicide of newly wedded Damien and Lucinda Knewsome.

Ex wedding planners Timothy and Amanda Jackson should by no means be approached.

If seen, call..

A Flight of fancy

The call came at about 06.30 I'd just got up and I could hear Jenny in the kitchen humming softly to herself as she pottered about making breakfast.

The call was from Frank and he sounded quite anxious.

'I know its your weekend off Matt but I need a favour'

An hour later I was on my way to the aerodrome, it was a big money job and there was no way I could turn it down. The Cessna 150 had been fuelled and loaded with its precious cargo and it sat on the small bay on the edge of the runway. I didn't know what the cargo was but that was no concern of mine. I had my instructions, Sandtoft to Lambley..flying time just under an hour.

*

A quick check of the engines systems and control surfaces and I got clearance from the small one- man air traffic control. All was clear for takeoff.

The short distance onto the main runway was bumpy but no more than I would expect given the slightly windy weather conditions.

Once on the runway I put the Cessna's nose over the centre line and a last check with air control confirmed my takeoff status.

My acceleration seemed smooth enough and I soon reached the desired speed of approx 68 miles an hour and carefully raised the elevators to commence my ascent.

The sky was a vivid blue with a smattering of white clouds and at 13,000 ft with a speed of just under 100 mph, the world was at my feet.

*

And then I woke up.

Wow, what a dream, it was so real, I actually felt as if I was flying even if I had never flown an aircraft in my life.

I shook myself from the fugue that had held me so deeply and then focused my eyes.

My bed was no longer a bed but what I took to be the cockpit of a small aeroplane. In front of me was a panel of meaningless switches, flashing lights and illuminated dials.

Ahead of me my sight was disrupted by the whirling of a powerful propeller.

And below me the ground was rushing up to welcome me.

Of course Jenny didn't hear my terrifying screams, she was miles away, humming softly to herself pottering about in the kitchen making breakfast.

Inculpate

1843.

I hadn't been consciously looking that particular day but on reflection I suppose that was the way it was going to eventually happen. I had been wandering around aimlessly when I found myself in a narrow unfamiliar street lined with shops and businesses of all descriptions. The few people that walked the uneven pavements paid little or no interest in the opened doorways that were the darker shadows in the day's light. I too had been a mere pedestrian until my eyes were drawn to the large bay fronted window and then instantly to the object itself. I must have been standing, staring at it for a considerable time as I was vaguely aware that a number of people had passed by; some making low murmurings at having to walk around my stationary figure.

It could not be helped; I had eyes and mind only for the object nestling on the dusty shelving between the worthless bric a brac and time ravaged tomes.To have said that at that moment in time I was wholly transfixed would indeed have been a vast understatement. As for its authenticity I had no doubt, I had no need to inspect it closer, to weigh it in my hands to feel its...*essence.* It was it and I knew it.

*

The old withered man behind the counter smiled at my approach as if he had been expecting me, without uttering a word he silently made his way towards the shelves at the front of the shop. With a dexterity that belied his frail and skeletal appearance he hefted the object from the dust of the shelf and holding it firmly in his bony fingers he turned to face me. "I will wrap it"
He made his shuffling way back to the counter and from somewhere under its well worn

wooden surface he produced several sheets of crumpled brown wrapping paper and a ball of twine. Laying the object on top of the uppermost sheet he proceeded with practised expertise to make the perfect package, the end product being neatly tied, sealed and compact.

He smiled again and held his hands out open palmed towards his endeavours. "There" Taking my proffered money was almost perfunctory to him; his eyes never once leaving the item of our transaction. And then I was back in the street, the object of my unintended but essential diversion clasped firmly in both hands. All was eerily quiet, the pavements void of life and the light now faded to grey, the doors of the buildings bar none, closed. If I had taken the time or felt the inclination to retrieve my watch from my waistcoat I would have seen that I had been over two hours in making that one purchase. I made my way home, a different person than had earlier left it - I have to confess Mr. Josiah Bradshaw Wentworth was no longer a person of whom you would like to have in your company.

2008.

"Will you take 15?"

"18"

The smell of frying onions prevailed, turning my stomach over as I stood in the damp long grass in front of the precariously sagging bench. On the bench's surface were all manner of articles, from discarded toys, clothing, hopeful objet d'art and dog eared books to old rusted and worn tools. At its centre causing no doubt the sagging and obviously the sellers main attraction was a pair of stag's antlers mounted on polished wood, majestic in their appearance, deeply sad in their demise. All of these items held no or little interest to me apart from...the one I had been sent for...

"Go on then I'll take 17"

The gnarled skinned man with the chunky silver bracelet dangling like a ship's anchor from his wrist picked up my purchase from the array on his bench with one hand...and took my proffered money with the other.

"Want a bag gov?"

"No thank you"

I caught the end of a fleeting grin on the seller's face and then with a combined sense of immense relief and unbelievable exultation the pendant was mine.

*

*Attached to an old and badly frayed leather strap by a tarnished but nevertheless solid silver clasp, the heavy forged bronze 'face' looked up at me from the palm of my hand. The eyes were empty, soulless, blind but yet all seeing, the mouth wide open as it had been and would be for all eternity frozen in a silent scream. I tore my eyes from the stare that had viewed the world contemptuously from at least since the 2nd century and slowly almost reluctantly turned the pendant over. The letters of the inscription were impossibly prominent, unsullied by a million curious fingers, they stood proud and obstinately legible, time had not been allowed to diminish their existence......***eram quod es, eris quod sum.*** The pendant and all that went with it was finally mine.*

Part Two

1844.

It was a den of iniquity if ever there was one, certainly not a place for a Gentleman of my breeding, within its walls all manner of cutthroats, thieves and vagabonds. Hence the attraction on that fateful day - it was more than my mortal self could resist.

"The name sir is Wentworth, Josiah Wentworth and you'd do well to remember it"

The Innkeeper was indeed a rapscallion, a man of far lesser breeding than I, a man that should without doubt count himself fortunate to be in my company, so his refusal to serve me another beverage was an insult of the highest order.

"You will replenish my glass and in haste sir or woe betide you sir" My words were slurred I admit but nonetheless comprehensible. Her cackle of a laugh resounded shrilly in the confinements of the Inn drawing amused glances from all and sundry.

"Give me another drink 'arry for the love of jesus, ee don't mean any 'arm, do ya luv?" The woman had appeared at my side as if from nowhere, her body was pressed to mine at such close proximity that I could smell the intoxication on her breath. She turned to me, a salacious grin spreading across her lips, her breasts almost completely exposed at her bodice. I had not envisaged this aside but I would not discourage it either. Most of the room's dubious occupancy had been alerted to my presence, eyes and ears following intently every scene...*a vaudeville act free of entrance fee.*

The Innkeeper put his drying towel over one shoulder and leant with both hands on the counter. He was talking to the lady but his eyes were on mine.

"We don't need 'is sort in 'ere Rosie"

"ee only wants a drink, don't ya mister"

The woman's hand had strayed to my crotch, her lips not a whisker from mine.

"Gonna buy the lady a drink, mister?" I had raised my glass as if giving an imaginary toast, a flamboyant gesture that brought more than a chuckle from the observing ensemble.

"Furnish the lady with another gin you scoundrel and whilst you are at it... "The Innkeeper made no move. I turned to the heavily powdered face of the lady and despite myself I could not suppress the wide smile on my face.

"Mine host seems reluctant to be compliant my dear, maybe we should seek another establishment...."

I let the suggestion drift away into the rancid smoke filled air to be assimilated by our uninvited audience. All bar none now were in full attendance. I placed one arm over the lady's shoulder and the other held my empty glass on the counter's surface. A mere shuffle of my weight gave away the level of my intoxication, as did, much to my annoyance, the slur in my words.

And then the lady was nestled further into my body, her lice laden, matted hair against my jowl, a leg between mine.

"Come on 'arry just one more and then I promise I'll.....I cut her off in midstream. "Replenish my drink, you wastrel and no more of your dalliance.... and one for..." My pause was deliberate but the irony was wasted on all.... "The lady" The Innkeeper was nothing if not persistent.

"I will ask you to leave my premises at once sir" In a room now filled with encouraging asides and sneering innuendoes my blood was hot, my hackles raised. I turned to look down at the lady's heavily made up eyes, seeing for the first time the shame and desperation set deep within them, for a fleeting moment I held a compassion for her...and then it was gone.

"Did you hear what that wretched imbecile uttered my dear lady, he has requested, nay demanded that I, Josiah Wentworth, a Gentleman of great standing in the community......a gentleman of a status the like of which he could never hope to ever attain in his squalid, worthless lifetime, he has demanded that I vacate his rat infested Inn - the effrontery of the man, I have a good mind to..." My words were garbled, disjointed, as if spoken by someone other than myself ...and then the room began to spin, my ears filled with the sounds of raucous, vicious laughter...jeering, mocking...everything before my eyes became a blur of bloated faces with staring eyes and mouths full of decayed stubs of grey jagged teeth...and then from somewhere a thousand miles away I was vaguely aware of a high pitched and heinous scream cut off almost instantly by the sound of snapping bone and choked into silence by a deep throated gargling. Instantly the dead weight of the woman was hanging limply by her disconnected head in the crook of my arm. A wave of disgust flitting across my senses I opened my elbow and let the body drop to the floor at my feet, I had further and far more pressing business to attend to. With unworldly strength I reached across and grabbed with both hands the Innkeepers lapels, in one fluid snatching and twisting movement I had the struggling man on his back on the counters surface. I placed an arm across his chest and held his upper body down, his spine bent double under the weight of his unsupported legs. I placed my lips against his ear and whispered what would be my last congenial words to him.

"You Sir were given ample opportunity to be obliging with me and you chose to be everything but"

With his face in such close proximity to mine his loud shouts of protestations were an irritating distraction that needed urgent addressing. I lowered my head closer to his and sank my teeth into the soft flesh of his cheek, tearing out as large a piece of meat as I could muster. I spat the bloody mass back onto what was left of his upturned face. The man's shouts became no more than a bubbling confusion of expelled air, his struggles intensified but my resolution was omnipotent. Satisfied with my work so far I reached for my empty glass and shattered it against the hard edge of the counter, happy with the results I plunged the jagged shards deep into the man's neck, hacking in a zigzag motion and observing closely the warm blood from his throat spurting up to drench the thick cotton of my coat sleeve. The room was suddenly filled with feral screams and frantic movements, but my concentration was not to be disturbed. Again and again I thrust my improvised weapon into the yielding flesh, exposing bone, tearing at sinewy ropes of scarlet tissue until it came away from muscle, my overwhelming intent to remove the offending head

altogether...just before the policeman's

truncheon

put an abrupt end to my joyous activities I felt

at my own neck for its presence...I went to the

floor and unconsciously in the happy

knowledge that the pendant was indeed still

adorning my person.

Part Three

1845.

"wot ya got there skinner?"

"thought it was money for a bit then, just a

scrap o' paper wi letters an all on it"

"Old lordy must a ritten it"

"ain't no good to im now is it skinner?"

"spose not"

Outside and silhouetted black against the blue

skies they are preparing my gallows. In the

mornings I listen to the birds singing until the men start with their hammering, their cursing. When the shadows lengthen, darken and meld into black, I await the inevitable visitation of my tormentors. This now is my only measure of time. Sleep is no longer a comfort permitted to me, no longer a release; I await with desperation the insanity that is imminent and already manifesting itself within me with the hope it will bring a merciful end to my suffering. I have abandoned all hope of forgiveness from my God, for if I cannot forgive myself, I have no right to ask it of him. The pendant is inculcated of all my inexplicable deeds; I know this to be true without a shadow of a doubt. But it was I who sought it; it was I who coveted it. God, I beg you to reconsider and have mercy on my soul.

J.B. Wentworth.

Part Four

2003

"A Mr. Simonds rang while you were out pet; he said he'd ring again later". Sally was in the back garden, a clothes peg held between her teeth, a yellow plastic laundry basket under one arm. He had been loading up his van with the emulsion and primer for the Barrets job and the sound of the kids shouting to each other across the street almost drowned out Sally's voice.....all he caught was ' *Simonds*' ...... *it was enough.* He pushed the vans doors shut and walked across to where she was hanging out the washing and peered over the fence at her.

'Did he leave a message?"

"Said he'd call back".

"Did he leave a number?"

He winced and almost swore aloud as a football smashed into the fence at his side.

"Oi watch it you kids"

A timid 'sorry' was uttered from the ball retriever and the boy was away back across the road before he could say another word. He looked back at his wife; she was on her way back into the house through the rear door, the empty laundry basket now sitting on top of the glass patio table.

"Did he leave a ..."

"Said he'd call back" And then she was gone.

*

It was a big job and the tender for it was put in, in haste and with not much hope, so when Sally mentioned the council man's name his heart skipped a beat. He checked his old army watch, should he go round to his office now?

No, he had the Barret job to finish and maybe Simonds only wanted to rub his nose in it and tell him his tender had been laughed at. He made his way back to the van, opened the driver's door, sat and absently watched the kids. *If the job had been given to him he would...no, he just didn't get that lucky.* His *'cutting in'* for the rest of that day left a lot to be desired.

The huge stone walled building was well over two hundred years old, situated in the middle of the city and boarded up for the past thirty or so years it had become a target for vandalism and graffiti artists. A short concrete path strewn with empty beer cans and old newspapers led to the main doors, they both stood looking up at the words that were etched high into its drab grey walls *'Magistrates Court'*.

"Used to be the main police cells as well as the Magistrates Courts"

As he spoke Simonds took a heavy bunch of keys from his coat pocket and slotted the largest of them into the lock, at first the door refused to open but a bit of persuasion from the council man's shoulder and they were in. Simonds voice echoed in the interior's vast emptiness.

"Bet they've had some real wrong'uns in 'ere over the years"

Rays of light from the gaps in the boarded windows cut into the shadows and tiny dust mites danced in the limelight.

"Murderers, rapists, town planner's"

He was talking as he walked to the side wall and threw a switch. The dust mites performance came to an abrupt ending. They were standing in what must have been the entrance hall, a damp musty smell prevailed and for the first time since 'winning' the job he began

to have some serious reservations. The plaster and rendering in some areas was flaking away from the walls and years of tallow smoke from a million candles had yellowed and scored the original paintwork. The wood around the large bay windows had been subjected to layer upon layer of gloss making them almost impossible to open and the ceilings were high enough to warrant the need for scaffolding. In his eagerness to get the job he must have overlooked these *'slight problems'*.

Simonds left the main room and disappeared down a corridor, he followed the sounds of the man's footfalls in a subdued silence. "They don't build them like this anymore do they Mr. Chidlow?"

He barely heard the others words, his *professional eye* had taken over and as he walked from room to room his mind was busy timing the work and estimating materials....something he should have done properly before.

"You look bemused Mr.Chidlow?"

Bemused wasn't the word he would have chosen but...They had entered what looked like a large storage area, numerous boxes of dog eared paperwork; clip files, books and other office paraphernalia were strewn all around in an untidy shambles. Simonds was speaking again.

"Of course the Council will foot the bill for the skip which has already been ordered but as per our agreement Mr. Chidlow, it will be your responsibility to clear this...." the man paused before adding "this unwanted material prior to redecoration"

He nodded mutely; he had obviously missed that bit in 'our agreement'. Before he knew it Simonds had handed him the bunch of keys all labelled up with their appropriate designations ("we have spares of each at the council's offices") and was on his brisk way to the exit.

He listened for the front door to be closed and as the echo of it died down sat heavily on the nearest dust covered box. He would start with this lot first thing in the morning, the Barrets job could wait.

*

Reached by a little used gravel drive hidden in shadows between the ends of two terraced houses, the small area at the back of the building was a jungle of overgrown weeds and nettles enclosed by a rusted wire fence. In the fence was a gate and holding that gate closed a rusted chain with an equally rusty but formidable looking padlock. He had no need to check for the keys, the weight of them in his jacket pocket was enough. He fished them out , unlocked the padlock and rear doors and in no time at all he was standing completely alone inside the massive building, listening to the eerie silence that only empty buildings can produce. By midmorning he had all the primers and his dust sheets in the main hall ready to begin and that's when the shouting and banging on the front doors began.

"Where do you want the skip mate?"

The decorating would have to wait; he had spent all the previous evening at home working out his plan of action and had totally forgotten the room that was full of boxes.

.....the manner in which you committed these heinous crimes is far beyond the comprehension of any god fearing man, the consequences of your actions leaving two people dead and in the most horrendous manner imaginable, namely butchery...I am at a loss as to what drove you to such abominable deeds, a man of your impeccable breeding ...it is therefore my duty in the name of the law to sentence you to death for the crimes that you have so wilfully and cold-bloodedly perpetrated. You will be taken from this court of law henceforth to a place of execution and at an allotted time be hung by the neck until dead....and may God have mercy on your soul...

He looked again at his watch, then a glance at the night sky outside the window confirmed it, it really was eight thirty. It had not been his intention to rummage through the material in the boxes but that was exactly what he found he was doing, for over four hours he had been taking them one by one to the skip but not before picking out individual files to look through. He had been fascinated by what were obviously the court records of cases and trials. The yellowed sheet of paper now in his hands was representative of the previous accounts but unlike the others had been sealed in a buff coloured file with a strange looking (for want of a better description) *medallion*.

He stood and stretched, the air in the building had turned cold and his stomach reminded him that he had not eaten all afternoon. Only a few boxes to go and he could do them tomorrow, this time he told himself he would be less curious and more industrious and get the job done. He made his way to the main hall, switched off the building's lights and locked the main doors; outside he found the padlock where he had left it on the gravel and locked it back in place. He put the keys in his jacket pocket, careful not to put them in the same pocket as he had the medallion. He hadn't stolen it; it was, after all, destined for the skip.

Part Five

2008.

The queue for' checking in' was painfully slow and a family of small children immediately behind me were noisy and boisterous, playing on my already taunt nerves. I had taken out my book at least three times but had found myself reading the same paragraph over and over again without a word going in. In the taxi to the airport I had another fleeting desire, stronger than the one yesterday but again just manageable.

....put your arm over the back of the seat, take his neck from behind and I will lend you the strength to break the bones in his vertebrae as if you were snapping sun dried twigs...

By the time we reached the airport dropping off point the urges had dissipated, the sensations calmed, the taxi driver no longer a focus for my...my...*attention..* Now getting closer and closer to the checking in desk, my blood was warming, my skin tingling, something in my mind becoming unhinged...*if that little boy accidentally bumps into me again I am going to force my finger deep into his eye sockets and..*I felt my hand tighten on the handle of my one and only suitcase and could visualise what was hidden deep inside the bundle of my clothes. Please God do not let the uniformed people detect it... or me.

The hand on my shoulder made me physically jump.

"Mr. De'Angelis?"

I turned to face a man in uniform, I stuttered my reply...."Yes"

"Yours I believe?"

The man was holding up before me a travel bag....my travel bag. I must have left it on a seat in the airport lounge somewhere; I took it thanking him profusely. He was gone; my heart resumed its natural beat, I wiped the beads of sweat from my brow with the back of my hand. I checked the departure board again. Flight IT3045...Lazio...15.45 hrs.From the airport at Lazio it is but a short journey to Frascati the place of my birth....and then on to my final destination deep in the Alban Hills........Tusculum, "e mio Dio venire con me" (and may my God go with me).

Part Six

2003

There was no sound, only the clicking sensation against the pad of his thumb as he popped closed the last fastening on his camouflage jacket. He bent to pick up the assault rifle, palmed the loaded magazine into the breach then slipping the leather strap on his shoulder he rested the heavy weapon against his chest. Outside the clouds had dispersed and the sun had begun to dry the grass lawns, pathways and roads, the smell of the recent rain was earthy, sweet.
Max Phillips was the first to die; he had his newspaper from the local shop wedged under

his arm and was leaning his bicycle against the wall of the council house he and his wife had lived in for over thirty two years. The first of two rounds took away most of his right shoulder. The second round entered his head just below his right ear taking parts of his brain through the exit wound to splatter red and grey on the wall behind.

Alison Bartlet was next. She looked up from the pushchair to see the man in army dress raise his arms to chest level and then her world ceased to exist. David Sullivan changed from first to second and then his windscreen shattered into a million ice cubes, his vision blurred red before the car mounted the curb and the skin on his face melted. All was silent for the man as he rounded the corner. The people looked at him open mouthed before the fire burst from somewhere in his hands and their bodies went down before him, like the tall hay he scythed as a young man in the fields, the bodies went down before him. In the window the woman with the white hair, a line of dotted holes in the plaster and then her head exploding in a ball of blood. Running, the figure in the raincoat, dancing as he ran now, the bullets slamming into his back, his folded umbrella discarded in the road behind. All was silent.

And then the man was in his van, the smell of paint reminding him of something, something a long way away, squeezing a solitary tear from a stone eye and then the cold steel was in his mouth.

Part Seven

He knew there was something big going on before he had reached Palmer Road, on the

Southcote Estate. Police cars and ambulances had raced past him and there were more and more vehicles in their wake. At five o'clock in the morning the activity was to say the least unusual.

"Looking for Palmer Road mate"

The voice was male, somewhere behind him. He was fumbling in his bag for another bundle of letters; he shouldn't have had to do that, he was getting irritated. Dennis Willis was usually a methodical, meticulous man; his letters were always neatly arranged so he could pick them out in order, in the dark, and without having to use his Post Office issue torch. This morning was different, disrupting, and because of that, his letter bundles were in disarray. He ignored the driver in the car at the kerb alongside him until the man was forced to ask his question again.

"Palmer Road mate?"

And still Dennis Willis would vent his annoyance, five o 'clock....in the morning was his time, had been for over twenty seven years...

"Sorry, are you talking to me?"

It was then Dennis saw the lady, she must have excited the car from the roadside and was making her way around its bonnet towards him. Dennis stiffened, his annoyance dissipated, the lady was going to speak to him, he could feel the blushing starting already.

"Excuse me sir but I am from the Reading Evening Post, have you seen anything, heard anything this morning?"

"A lot of people and cars going about"

Dennis had spoken the words before he realised he'd opened his mouth; the lady was getting closer, too close. The man in the car spoke.

"Come on Janice, I can see lights over there, I told you, all we needed to do was follow....."

Dennis was speaking again, pointing a finger on an outstretched arm.

"Down there, second left, down Southcote Lane, past St Davids...." The lady was stepping away, she smiled. Dennis's shirt collar felt tight all of a sudden, his blush deepened and the morning for him had only just begun.

A few of them had finished before him and the noise in the sorting office was deafening.

"ere ee is"

Dennis had been dreading his return, more so this morning than ever before.

"What the hell's going on up on your route Dillis?"

They had always called him Dillis, Dennis had read somewhere that if you had a nickname it meant you were popular.

"Fucking blue and white tape everywhere, ambulances and coppers cars, they must have half the fucking force out there"

The voices were coming from all over the now crowded office. Dennis knew the faces of the speakers but not the names. He had never needed to know the names.

"For fuck sake Dillis, you go round all day with your fucking eyes shut?"

Dennis hated the swearing.

"They didn't let me post these and they kept asking me questions"

Dennis was holding up his half empty sack.

"Who wouldn't let you post them?"

Another voice from the crowd.

"The policemen at the barrier in Palmer Road".

Now there was laughter.

"Typical of old Dillis, fucking world war three breaks out and ee's worried that he had to bring his fucking letters back"

More laughter...until.."Maniac loose out there, they reckon there are nine people dead and at least four critical".

The supervisor had just stepped through the large rubber doors at the entrance to the loading bay, a silence fell as his voice boomed authority. After a while someone managed to speak. "Christ in a tin 'at"

He put his bike in the shed and made his way through the narrow alley between the houses to the front door; the neighbour's dog barked its usual warning from the other side of the fence as he went. It had just begun to rain; he had already made up his mind, *no fishing for him today*. Mother was in the kitchen and the smell of bacon tugged at his stomach. Alice Willis cracked two eggs into the frying pan and wiped spattered fat off her chin with the back of her ample right arm.

"...and don't be treading all that mud through the house"

Dennis pulled off his boots and hung his jacket on its hook on the back of the kitchen door. He sat down at his place at the table and ran his hands palm down over the plastic red and white chequered table cover.

"Some people got killed up in the Southcote Estate earlier this morning Mother"

Alice put the plate in front of her son and turned back to her stove. A shrill whistle and a jet of steam added more hot moisture to an already a damp room. Alice pulled the top off the kettle's spout and turned down the gas under it.

"Do you want tea?"

She always asked Dennis that, and Dennis always said '*yes please*' but on this occasion he had something to say that was completely different.

"They reckon nine got killed".

For the first time since Dennis entered the kitchen Alice turned to look at her son.

"Who got killed, Dennis, where?"

"Somewhere down Palmer Road, can't be sure whereabouts, they wouldn't let me all the way down and it's a long road"

Mrs Willis crossed her arms against her chest and let out a huge sigh, when she spoke it was with undisguised irritation.

"Dennis, what in the Lord's name are you talking about?"

Dennis put his knife and fork down, he had been rehearsing his story all the way home from the Post Office. And after he'd told her it, he would give her the thing he had found lying on the ground in Palmer Road.

Part Eight

2008.

"I know you have been wanting to visit for a long time now honey, you have a lovely few days and don't worry about me"

Miranda's words came back to me as the aircraft's wheels touched down on Italian soil. I had not been 'home' for over twenty eight years and I had already begun to wish I was not on my way there now. I was remarkably calm as I went through the security and customs at Ciampino Airport; the wait for my suitcase from the carousel was short and uneventful...and then I was out into the dry heat of Italy and into the dusty taxi. As we drove off through the outlying suburbs of Rome, vague memories of playing as a barefooted child in the sun baked streets flitted across my mind. I could hear the sound of my mother's voice as she called me and my brothers into supper..

" Giorgio, Ruggiero, Pio, Lucca, Donato è il momento di gcome in miei bambini per la cena"

And then the taxi began to climb the Alban Hills and closer to Frascati a different sound from my mother came to my ears....her screams as his fists beat into her....

"20 € si prega di"

The driver was holding open the door, my travel case in his brown bony hand.

"Siamo arrivati Frascati"

The house hadn't changed at all..it still had the dark silence that my mother had bestowed on it all those years ago...and he was standing in the doorway, his arms outstretched his eyes anywhere but at mine.

"Benvenuto figlio a casa e stato un lungo periodo di tempo"

My father had aged considerably, but his embrace belied his appearance, it was strong, almost crushing and yet somehow as cold as marble.

"*It has* been a long time, father, it is nice to visit" I lied.

For a while I could think of nothing else to say and I stumbled over my Italian, it had been years since I had spoken it.

"Si prega di padre può parlare Englese"

I asked my father to speak in English; his disapproving frown could be translated in any language, he ignored my request.

"Offendi il tuo luogo di nascita mio figlio, non si aspettano che io faccia altrettanto" He was an Italian and so was I, by birth at least, as far as he was concerned I was insulting my mother tongue. I looked into his cold ice blue eyes and in an instant the memories came flooding back.

...the whole village had turned out, all in black, heads down in shadows under the hot Frascati sun...my mother's coffin carried by my elder brothers...my father drunk on cheap vino screaming obscenities as the cortege passed him by on the gravel path to the cimitero....

"Prendere la prostituta a terra e seppellirla in profondità"

(Take the whore to the ground and bury her deep)

"Spero che il diavolo stesso scricchiolio delle ossa e bevande suo sangue"

(I hope the devil himself crunches on her bones and drinks her blood)

"Voi non siete figli miei, siete il vostro madri delle spore"

(You are no sons of mine; you are your mothers spore)

The sounds drifted back to the closed side of my mind.

And then the man that was my father was staring, defiant eyes that seemed to read my every thought.

"It was by my hand that Natalia died Donato but I did not mean to kill her, I have prayed to God that you and your brothers will someday understand that"

His English was faultless, his eyes softer but his words held not a trace of remorse.

"What of your brothers Donato? I hear nothing from them all this time"

How could I tell my father that his sons only wished him dead, they had witnessed much of what I was too young to understand?

The silence that lingered for far too long between us could have been an eternity and when he finally spoke again my father was once again Italian.

He held out a leather skinned hand palm up to me and his other hand moved to his neck, his thumb and fingers forming a large V.

"Dammi il medaglione" Give me the medallion.

Part Nine

2003.

"Bloody dog along Gainsborough Road wants putting down"

Alice was upstairs in the bathroom going through the dirty linen basket; she heard the front door go but ignored it, Dennis was due home, she put the scissors down on top of the pile of clothes at her feet and cocked her head.

"Got to the gate and it came at me like a bloody....Mother?"

Dennis raised his voice and his head to peer up the darkened stairwell; it was only two thirty in the afternoon but already the day's light was diminishing, Alice would not put the house lights on until it was absolutely necessary.

"Don't swear Dennis"

Her voice came to him and it carried a tone with it that Dennis immediately recognised; chastising, admonishing.

"Why the hell do people keep dogs like that?" As he spoke Dennis made his way into the living room, inside the door his breath caught in his throat and he felt an overwhelming urge to defecate where he stood. Screen down in a sea of shattered glass on the carpet before him lay the television, its wires trailing from it like black and white intestines. To one side of the room the sofa vomited its internal filling through large lacerated slits in its leather surface and turning his head he saw the curtains hanging from their broken rails in shredded ribbons. The overhead light had been torn from the ceiling and was dangling by its flex, tiny specks of white dust from the cratered plaster above still settling on the floral patterned shades. In one corner of the room and barely recognisable the display cabinet had been upturned, its wooden panels splintered and hacked into firewood and its china and silver contents strewn about like abandoned and trampled confetti. Dennis stood in stunned silence, trying to make sense of the chaos that met his eyes in whatever direction he looked. And then a terror stricken scream tore from his throat..."Mother"

He took the stairs two at a time with the echo of his own uncontrollable yells bouncing from the walls of the narrow staircase...."Mother are you all right, Mother where are you?"

At the top of the stairs on the tiny landing he almost lost his balance as he threw himself against the door of his Mothers bedroom, it came open without resistance and he only just managed to prevent himself from falling head first onto the unmade bed. He placed one hand against the wall to steady himself and that's when the overpowering stench hit him, gagging and cloying he fought the immediate impulse to vomit. The source of the smell came to him as his foot slipped on

the faecal substance under his right foot and again he found himself struggling for balance. All around was in total disarray. His mother's dresser was tilted to one side, two of its legs broken and useless beneath it, on the carpet lay empty scent bottles, her open and disgorged jewellery box and next to that her set of silver hairbrush and mirror....all bent, twisted and smashed.

"Mother" He was shouting as he turned to leave the room, he slipped again and grabbed at the door frame, the excrement on his shoes leaving long staining streaks in the once pristine carpet.

"Mother, where are you..?"

She was standing at the far end of the landing, naked from the waist down, smiling, the scissors in her right hand glinting dully in the failing light and one of his shirts cut to ribbons in her left.

"Dennis, what have I told you about taking your shoes off before you come upstairs?

Alan Broadbent Operations Manager at the town's Royal Mail Office could barely believe what he was hearing, until Reggie Davies, his shift Supervisor caught his attention.

"It all happened on Dennis's route"

Alan raised his eyebrows, a look of comprehension spreading across his face; he put the phone's receiver back to his mouth.

"Ok Dennis, don't worry, if it's more than five days you need to get yourself a Doctors Certificate, you do know that don't you?"

Alan nodded silent agreement on the telephone a few times and then...

"Right oh, Dennis, have a good rest and we will see you back here in a few days"

Alan hung up. In the silence of the office that followed, the two men looked at each other across the desk.

"Never known Dennis to phone in sick in all the years I've been here"

Alan still had a hand on the receiver in its cradle. Reggie looked at his boss, pushing the memory of the car accident and his brother's death to the back of his mind.

"Something like what happened to all those poor bastards in Palmer Road gotta have some sort of effect on you I suppose"

"Yeah, I suppose so," said Alan Broadbent, Operations Manager.

"Better get somebody to cover his route"

Dennis held the receiver up at his ear long after the click told him Mr. Broadbent had hung up. His skin felt clammy at the back of his neck and his hands were shaking uncontrollably. Dennis had never lied to Mr. Broadbent before; Dennis could not remember lying to anyone before. Alice was sleeping on the settee in the lounge; she had been since about one o'clock that morning, it was now just before five. Dennis had been up all night scrubbing the bedroom carpet with disinfectant; he had opened all the windows but the house got very cold so he was forced to close them again. He had managed to get his mother down stairs, clean her up and dress her in her night wear and she had been completely silent whilst he did it, more than silent...*vacant.* The only time she made any attempt to move was when he tried to take the thing from around her neck, the thing he remembered he had given her, the thing he found in Palmer road. She groaned and placed her cold bony hand over his.

"Leave that be Dennis" He left it.

Dennis tried not to look at the mess all around, the broken furniture, the smashed ornaments. Dennis tried hard not to think about it all. He would fix it all and then no-one would know. He thought about calling the Doctor but then what would happen if he did? Maybe they would take his mother away; he would be on his own. No, no need for all that rubbish. Dennis would fix it all and nobody would know. Mr. Broadbent had said...

"Right oh, Dennis, have a good rest and we will see you back here in a few days" A few days...Nobody would know.

"Dennis"

He must have dropped off on the wooden chair he had been sitting on, her voice from the other room made him start.

"Dennis"

"Yes Mother"

He was amazed at how croaky his voice sounded; he could not get the taste of disinfectant from his throat.

"Get in here, now Dennis"

Dennis got to his feet and made his way through the open door to the lounge. The heavy glass fruit bowl caught him on the side of his head and sent a flash of blinding white light streaking across his eyes.

Part Ten

1190 A.D.

Tomasi stood on the banks of the Tuscus Amnis watching his father Domenica pulling tighter the binds across Gioacchino's naked chest. He watched as the leather bound boulders were then tethered to his brother's ankles and the wooden stake passed through the loops of twine at his shoulders. His brother lay on his back, his unblinking

eyes looking directly into the fire of the noonday sun, a wide lunatic smile stretching the skin on his burnt lips. In the distance, high in the Alban Hills their mothers wailing had subsided somewhat but was still audible; carried down to them on shimmering waves of unyielding heat; Raffaella would not interfere but she would not witness either. From across the river came the foetid stench of the many slain by Gioachino, their bodies buried in shallow graves, growing shallower by the minute as the hot wind toyed with the thin covering of dust and sand laid upon them. Domenica and Tomasi had done all they could for the dead, alone as they were, the others of the village having already fled from the coming of Barbarossa's Army. Soon Tusculum would be destroyed, along with it Gioachino's memory.

Lapis supra lapidem non remasit

'Not a stone upon a stone remains'.

But first. Domenico took the chainless pendant from the pouch in his tunic and bent over the bound and writhing body of his eldest son. Tomasi knelt, a knee at either side of Giochino's head and placed his hands on his brother's chin and forehead holding his head as still as he could. With powerful gnarled and calloused fingers Domenico forced the pendant into the man's mouth, pushing it past his biting teeth and deep into his throat. With straining biceps father and son took the weight of Giochino's retching body and along with the boulders carried it down the inclining bank towards the rushing waters of the Tuchus Amnis.

"Prendere il male con voi per la vostra morte Giochino"

(Take the evil with you to your death Giochino")

Domenico's eyes had drifted to the rivers far bank and the tiny mounds just visible in the hot sands, his voice a whisper to the dead.

"Per un 'po sono troppo tard- Che gli dei mi perdoni"

(For some I am far too late, may the Gods forgive me).

Domenico and Tomasi tossed Giochino's body into the currents and spat in the waters after him. And Raffaella's scream rose to a crescendo and echoed through the shadows of the distant hills. Long after the flesh of Giochino's body had been devoured by the grateful creatures of the Tuchus Amnus and her waters had washed his bones to no more than grains of sand...it would be her own turn to die. *The earth itself moved and took the mighty river bed from under it, leaving the sun to slowly, patiently, drink her waters in the searing heat of a thousand, thousand days. In the baked and crusted rock that was now the shadow of the Tuchus Amnus a single glint of gold caught his eye. He bent to pick it up. He had been born too.*

Part Eleven

2003.

Dennis took his hand away from the side of his head and looked at the deep red blood smeared over its palm;... *It wasn't the type of blood you got from a paper cut or from shaving, it was...*He needed to steady himself, his legs could not hold his weight, he placed his other hand on the wall at his side and leant his head into his shoulder... and that's when the pain came, in one sudden nauseating wave, the pain came. From his temple across his cheek bone to the base of his jaw a throbbing, shooting agony that brought tears to his eyes and made whooshing sounds in his ears.

"What the hell...?" the words came from his mouth on a jet of spittle.

Through blurred eyes he saw movement and then a sound registered somewhere in the peripheral of his brain.

"Dennis, are you alright darling, Dennis...?" And now there was a hand under his arm...

"Dennis, speak to me darling are you...?" She was leading him to the bed, almost stumbling as she angled her tiny body under his; he could feel her warm breath through the thin material of his damp shirt.

"Sit down here darling, I will get something to clean you up"

Alice had one arm around her son's lower back the other holding his blooded hand, *ballroom dancers, dancing a joyless foxtrot......* She helped her son lower himself on the edge of the bed and then turning her back on him walked towards the bedroom door; she stepped over the upturned fruit bowl on the carpet without a second glance and was gone.

"Sit still, Dennis darling,mother will be back as"....her voice drifted away under the sounds of her footfalls descending the stairs.

Dennis sat on the edge of the bed staring at the fruit bowl, the one that until now had stood empty on the downstairs window sill for as long as he could remember...Alice was back in the room; spilling water from a plastic basin in her hands, under her arm was clenched tightly a clean towel.

"You poor thing...." as she spoke she sat next to her son on the bed and started to dip the towel into the basin.

"There, there we will soon get you cleaned up in..." Alice did not finish her sentence, with a look of deep concern she started dab at the side of her son's head. Dennis flinched at first contact then fought to keep himself still; even speaking bought fresh pain to the raw wound, the growing bruise.

"Mother what happened....why did you throw that...?"

Alice's administration ceased abruptly, her hand with the wet and dripping towel hovering inches from Dennis's face...

"What?"

The word was spat rather than spoken, Alice got to her feet, the basin dropped from her hand spilling tepid water over Dennis's trousers and the bed's cover.

"What did you say Dennis?" Alice's face was contorted in rage, her fist white, the towel between her fingers sending more water squirting in tiny jets to the carpet.

"What did you fucking say you ..."

And then the chimes of the front door bell echoed, 'Waltzing Matilda' up the empty stairwell.

Dennis had thanked and not thanked the lady with the Conservative Party leaflet in her hand, ignored her gaze, focused on his bruised and cut temple and closed the front door.

He stood for a while looking at the back of the door, listening to the sound of the lady's footfalls as they grew fainter...he felt his mothers movements at his back as she stepped past him. He woke from his reverie and followed her into the lounge; it was a while before he spoke.

"I am going to call the Doctor Mother"

Alice did not respond, did not move, her eyes were fixed on something on the ceiling above her son's head.

"Mother I don't think you are well"

And then her eyes were on his, in his.

"Did you fancy her Dennis; did you like the look of that lady at the door?"

Dennis stared back at his mother, eyebrows raised, mouth open, wordless questions on his lips.

"Did you want to drag her inside and fuck her Dennis?"

Alice was standing in the centre of the room her fists clenched at her sides; she was running the tip of her tongue across her upper lip, a lewd grin spreading across her open mouth.

"Did you want to give her one Dennis?"

Laughter cracked like a whip from deep within her throat and Dennis's eyes were drawn to the pitter patter sounds of her urine hitting the carpet in heavy drops between her legs. And then as quickly as it started the laughter ceased and the grin on Alice's face was gone, replaced by a snarl, a feral snarl...her voice the hiss of a serpent.

"But of course Dennis dear, you couldn't possibly do that could you?"

As she spoke she took a step closer, her hands came up to each side of her cheeks and she cradled her chin in her upturned palms. Dennis could only stand and stare.

"My poor baby is frightened, isn't he?"

Another step closer and then another.

"People frighten you don't they Dennis, Dennis doesn't like people does he...especially ladies?"

And now Alice's arms were outstretched, her voice soft, her eyes misted with moisture.

"Come to your mother Dennis, I won't let them hurt you again"

Despite himself Dennis found himself stepping back...back from his own old and frail mother... The absurdity of his reaction was upon him immediately. He took two determined steps towards her, his voice was charged as he held his own arms out towards her shoulders.

"Mother I am going to get you into your bed and I am calling the Doctor now, you are not well"

The stinging slap almost took him off his feet and for a moment he was completely deaf in one ear, fresh pain flared up in his temple and a cold trickle of blood eased its way down his cheek. He fought to regain his balance and glimpsed his mother's lips moving but the sounds were just a distorted cornucopia, a thousand bells ringing shrilly in his head.

"For Christ's sake Mother" Dennis's hands were now over his ears trying to block out the string of obscenities that were now pouring from Alice's mouth.

She took a step towards her son; he could feel her spittle on his face.

"You are nothing but a fucking waste of a man Dennis...a disappointment to me, a disappointment even to that bastard of a father of yours....you are a fucking.."

It was then that Dennis hit her, a clenched fist that contacted with her cheek bone stunning her into instant silence and sending her flying backwards onto the bed.

*

"I am so sorry Mother...I am so.....I didn't mean to....I am so..." As he spoke the heavy sobbing shook his body catching his words in his throat, the wound to his temple had intensified and become a heavy cloud of a headache.

"I really didn't mean to do that mother I...."

They were sitting side by side on the bed, mother and son, Alice had one arm arched over Dennis's shoulders, the fingers of her other hand gently stroking the side of his tear stained face, his head against her bosom.

"I don't know what happened mother, I just don't know...."

For a while the only sound in the room apart from Dennis's abating weeping was the tick, tocking of an alarm clock coming from somewhere on Alice's bedside cabinet, when Alice did eventually speak, Dennis felt the arm around his shoulder stiffen and the fingers at his face scratch.

"You hit me"

Dennis was aware of his mothers quickening heartbeat, her shallow, gasping breath.

"You fucking hit me" She spoke as if the realisation had just occurred to her.

Now they were sitting apart facing each other, Alice's eyes wide in astonished anger, Dennis his hand back at his temple, mouth gaping in disbelief.

"You inadequate little bastard, you think you can hit your own mother and get away with it?" And then she was upon him, catching him completely unaware, her entire weight and with strength phenomenal, pushing him onto his back on the bed, tearing at his hair dragging her nails deep into his

scalp and then running her bony fingers down to dig into his eye sockets.

"You can't hit me you..., you can't hit me, you're snivelling a little..."

Her manic ranting deafened him as he felt her clamp her teeth onto the fleshy lobe of his ear, she bit down hard sending fresh new pain streaking through his body...a pain that filled his head with rage and the muscles in his arms with hot pulsating blood. Dennis gripped at his mother's flanks with both hands, lifted her body from his and with all his remaining strength threw her up and sideways to land with a sickening thump on the bedroom floor. For a while Alice lay motionless, winded, a low murmuring issuing from salivating lips that were crushed against the dry fabric of the carpet. Dennis elbowed his way up to a sitting position, put a hand to what remained of his ear, winced and wiped the blood on the beds counterpane. He looked down at the crumpled mess on the floor that was his mother, relieved to see the up and down motion of her ribs.

"I'm getting an ambulance mother I'm...going now"

He stood, his knees creaked and he felt warm blood drip down the side of his neck and under his shirt collar. He made his way to the bedroom door fighting the dizziness that had begun to blur his vision. He heard her before he had time to completely turn around; the china lamp struck a glancing blow against his shoulder and smashed into pieces against the jamb of the door. Dennis stepped and blindly grabbed at his mother's flailing arms, his fingers closed tightly on the neck of her clothes; ripping and tearing he pulled down hard in a desperate attempt to get her to the floor, *to subdue her.* Mother and son went down in a struggling tangle. And once there They lay together in a silence that was mutual and strangely subliminal.

It landed in a corner of the bedroom on top of a pile of clothes that were now nothing more than Alice's cut up rags, and under its own weight the medallion slipped into obscurity.

Part Twelve

2006

'I don't think we should bother to tip them do you?"

Monica was standing at the open front door watching the men loading the sack trucks into the back of the lorry, the one that had made the blatant pass at her was leaning against the cab lighting a cigarette. Behind her Michael was struggling up the bare wood stairs with the last of the (*bedroom*) tea chest in his arms, its sharp metal edges adding more scratches to his already bloodied skin.

"I shall be on the blower first thing to complain about them, that's for sure, the lazy...." He paused remembering his daughters in the room just off the landing,

"So and so's," he finished. His voice came to her as a series of disjointed grunts.

"Shut the door doll; let's get the last of it finished"

Monica shut the door, smiling at the sudden sound of Amy and Melissa's excited voices coming from one of the empty upstairs bedrooms.

"My rooms are bigger than yours cos I'm the oldest...."

She made her way around the furniture cluttered lounge into the kitchen and found the kettle.

"Coffee first?"

Michael had reached the bottom of the stairs for the umpteenth time that day...."Sounds great" He gestured with a finger up the stairwell...

"Listen to those two, do they ever stop squabbling?"

Monica smiled in reply.

*

Mummy and Daddy had been busy all day, they'd had hot dogs for dinner and mummy said they were sending out for a 'Chinese' later. Melissa was in her room reading....she said she was tired and wanted 'space'. Amy slipped quietly down the stairs; mummy was talking on the phone...in the lounge...

"We really are up to our ears in it mum......no the removal men were no good at..Michael's just popped out to get some light bulbs...can you believe it they took the light...the girls are fine mum they..."

Now Amy was in the kitchen going through the opened box labelled *'kitchen utensils'*

"....we'd love to mum but it will have to be late tomorrow...."

Amy found one, it was the old one mummy used to cut up Ben's food with, Amy thought for a while about Ben, his big floppy ears and....

".....ok mum, I will have lots to do....."

Amy held the knife behind her back with both hands....mummy would be finished on the phone soon, she wouldn't like it if she saw her with a knife..

"Yep, yep, I'll call later tonight...ok mum...love you too"

Amy was at the bottom of the stairs......

"Is that you darling...?"

"Yes mummy is just getting something..."

Amy ran up the stairs two at a time, the knife held tightly in her hand.

"Melissa"

Amy was standing outside Melissa's closed bedroom door, her voice a hushed whisper"

"Go away I'm busy"

Her sister's response came back curt and dismissive; the younger girl at the other side of the door shrugged it off.

"Melissa I've got something to show you"

"Amy go away"

Again Amy ignored her elder sister; her voice grew louder, more insistent.

"I've got something to show you"

A noise, a movement from inside the bedroom, Amy held her breath, the door creaked open and a shadowy face appeared in the gap.

"What?"

Melissa's curiosity had got the better of her.

"In my room"

The door opened fully and Melissa stood looking down at her little sibling.

"Amy, what do you want?"

Amy had turned her back and was walking across the landing to her own room, from downstairs the sound of a hover being switched on echoed up the carpet less wooden stairs.

"Amy?"

Melissa followed her sister, the exasperation in her voice now loud and clear. Amy stopped at her room's doorway and with a gesture of her hand waved her elder sister forward.

"This had better not be one of your silly games Amy

Inside the room Melissa turned around just in time to see Amy close the door. In her little sister's hand the knife looked enormous.

"Damn" Monica put her foot on the red button and the vacuum cleaner's whirring motor slowly died away, the knocking of the door taking its place as the only sound in the house.

"Damn" Monica repeated as she made her way out of the lounge to the landing.

"If you need yer window's cleaning love I'm yer man"

He was standing in the doorway holding out a piece of paper with one hand and doffing an imaginary cap with the other. Monica could not help but smile; she took the proffered paper and read the blue writing, *Malcolm Haines... Window Cleaner Extraordinaire.*

"Did for the last lot love and never a word of complaint"

Now he had his back to her and was on his way towards the gate and to the road beyond.

"Give us a call any time love" And he was gone

Monica stood in the doorway waiting for him to shout, Mr. Grimsdale but it never came....she closed the door, the smile on her face even wider.

"What are you doing Amy?"

The younger girl was standing with her back to the closed door; she raised the knife to her face and looked at it as if she'd never seen it before.

"Amy, what are you doing with that?"

Melissa's voice faltered as her eyes caught a glint of light from the knife's blade.

"Amy?"

Downstairs the sound of the vacuum cleaner died...and in the silence Melissa was immediately aware of her sister's footfalls as the younger girl began to walk hurriedly towards her...and then brushing against her shoulder, past her.

"Look Melly, look at this"

Amy was using the knife in her hand to point at the floorboards below the bedroom's only window. Melissa watched with growing curiosity as her sister went down on all fours to the floor.

"Look Melissa look", the child's voice was excited, insistent.

"Down"

Amy gestured with her hand and before she knew it Melissa was with her sister on her hands and knees on the floor.

"Look"

Melissa looked where Amy had the knife's tip hovering over a tiny gap in the wooden boards. At first all Melissa could see was splinters of freshly gouged wood, she bought her sister's eye up with her own.

"You wait until daddy sees that"

Amy let out a little frustrated sigh... and tapped the wooden floorboard with the blade.

"Look Melissa"

It was gold in colour and looked like the edge of a coin; it was wedged deeply between the floorboards and bore the fresh scratches of Amy's previous endeavours to gouge it out. Amy turned to her head to face her sister and spoke into her ear; her voice in the cold silence of the bedroom was one Melissa had never heard before.

"When I get it out it's, mine"

From downstairs came the sound of the vacuum cleaner starting up again, Amy's voice was easily audible over its distant droning and the tip of the knife in her hand waved within inches of her sister's face.

"It's all mine Melissa".

*

The office was on the first floor overlooking the car park at the rear of the school. Mrs Patterson had ushered them in and then bade them sit down on two chairs facing a large veneered desk. Michael and Monica exchanged a brief nervous glance and then they both watched as Mrs Patterson took her seat at the opposite side of the desk. Monica held the folded letter in her hand, it was damp with perspiration.

"Thank you for coming"

Mrs Patterson looked directly at Monica, pushed her glasses up to the bridge of her nose and was silent for a while as she formulated her words, when she finally spoke she had shifted her gaze to Michael, the head teacher wasted no time in preamble.

"We, meaning myself and my colleagues at the school, are concerned..." her pause was fleeting.. " *very,* concerned" she emphasised " about your daughters behaviour of late"

Monica made to speak but was immediately silenced by Mrs Patterson's singled handed gesture.

"I'm afraid we have major problems to resolve regarding Amy's conduct, it appears your daughter has not only been rude and disruptive in the classroom but I have heard from her tutors that she has made threats of a violent nature to her fellow pupils"

"She is seven years old"

Monica leaned forward in her seat and brushed her husband's hand of comfort forcefully from her shoulder as she spoke.

"She is only seven years old for Christ's sake; I cannot believe what has been said..."

She had the letter crumpled in the fist of her right hand and her already red swollen eyes were beginning to well with more tears.

"Mrs Rowland I can assure you that...."

It was Michael's turn to interrupt.

"My wife and I have read this letter over and over again and there must be some kind of mistake, maybe a little over exaggeration"

The head teacher's response was spoken through tight humourless lips.

"Mr Rowland I assure you Amy's behaviour has been completely unacceptable...*she has hit....she bit her finger....it took two teachers to....swore and spat at....*"

Mrs Patterson's words were a jumble of sounds as Monica tried desperately to ignore the images that were now so vivid in her mind...

....the torn sheets...the smashed ornaments....the bloodied remains of the goldfish trampled into the sodden fabric of the carpet...the excrement spread by tiny fingers all over the toilet's wall...

Michael was speaking... "She has always been a spirited young lady; maybe it's just the pressure of moving to a new school...a new environment..."

Monica was now shaking her head from side to side as if the movement would dislodge the tiny voice that was now ringing in her ears...*I don't want to mummy....you can't make me mummy...no, why should I...?"*

More words, this time from the lady teacher... *"She needs professional help....we at the school cannot be....the situation needs to be addressed without further delay....".*

Monica felt the vomit rise from deep in her stomach.... " *no mummy, I won't....no you can't make me..... nooooo....fuck you mummy*"

As the floor rose up to meet her, Monica was vaguely aware of Michael's hands grabbing at her flailing arms and the heavy desk between them tipping up crushing painfully against her and taking the skin from her knees. And then black.

"She's asleep"

"And Melissa?"

"In her room reading"

"Are you feeling better now?"

Monica ignored her husband's question; she was studying the label on the wine bottle clasped in her fingers.

"We have to talk about Amy, Mo, we have to get to the bottom of all this"

Monica was on her third glass of wine; her hands trembled as she topped up a glass that was only half empty.

"That won't help Monica"

Michael was sitting at the dining room table surrounded by what remained of the evening's meal; he was looking at Monica and shaking his head from side to side.

"It's helping me" Monica wiped her nose on the back of her sleeve and reached out to the coffee table for a letter she had read a thousand times she made to pick it up and then thought better of it.

"I will get tomorrow off and..."

Monica spoke over her husband's words.

"What is wrong with Michael, what is wrong with Amy?"

Her voice faltered and she wiped her nose on her sleeve again.

"It's something and nothing, change of school, making new friends, hormones"

Michael stood up slowly from the table and sat next to his wife on the couch; he made to put an arm around her but remembered her reaction in Mrs Patterson's office.

"She swore at me the other day"

Monica was looking at the tips of her fingers.

Michael poured himself a drink from the same bottle, emptying it.

"Kids pick it up at school Mo, you know that"

"She told me to fuck off"

Michael swallowed hard on his wine and turned to look at his wife with a stunned expression on his face.

Monica was staring into space and talking into the empty air.

"She killed the goldfish".

Fresh tears were in her eyes as she turned to face her husband, she spoke with what sounded like hysterical laughter cracking at her voice.

"She told me it had jumped out of its fucking bowl, the one it has been happily swimming about in for as many years as I can fucking remember and she tried to catch it but somehow managed to stamp it into fucking oblivion...a red bloody mess on the carpet Michael.....and do you know what was even worse than that Michael ?...shall I tell you what was even worse than that?..Amy was smiling as she told me....looking down at the mess that was the goldfish with a big...*ha ha look what I've done with a smile* on her face.

And now Monica's maniacal laughter turned completely to rasping sobs...

"She's spread shit all over the toilet walls, she's smashed all my.... and..."

It was then that the sobbing took all of her remaining breath and all Monica could do was weep, Michael put an arm around her shoulder, this time she did not flinch, he searched his mind for something to say and nothing came out.

"We should never have moved here"

His wife's voice was little more than a murmur from somewhere deep against his chest. Michael put a hand under Monica's chin and gently raised her face towards his.

"Oh come on Mo, moving here is hardly a reason to...."

Monica sat up and straightened her back, pulling herself away from Michaels embrace, her red eyes were wide, her nose and mouth wet with dribble.

"What did that estate agent say about the old woman and her son who sold us this place?"

"Oh for Christ's sake Mo..."

Michael got no further; Monica was tripping over her words, all rationale gone.

"The old lady went fucking mad..nearly killed him...that's why we got the place cheap...the son wanted rid of it and her...."

"Now that's enough Monica, you are upset, you are talking rubbish"

Michael was holding her by both shoulders gently shaking her....

"Now calm down Mo, for god's sake calm down and.."

"It's the thing she found"

Melissa was standing in the open doorway of the lounge, her bare feet just visible under the crumpled hem of her long pale blue nightdress; she stepped silently into the room out of the shadows of the dark landing and spoke again.

"The thing she found in her bedroom, in the crack in the floor"

*

"It is all to do with that thing mummy; Amy has been horrible to everybody since she found it"

"Come and sit over here Melissa"

Monica heard her husband's voice and felt his weight shift on the sofa; she had both hands at her face trying to dry tears with an already soggy tissue, her eldest daughter could not see that she had been crying. Melissa made her barefoot way slowly to the sofa and sat between her parents; she glanced up at the ceiling as if she had heard a noise and then her voice was a whisper...

"I helped her get it out with a knife..."

Melissa paused looking ruefully at her father...

"It's ok honey, what thing did you help Amy get..."

"It was a coin thing, a gold coin and it was stuck between the floorboards...Amy asked me to help her get it out...she had a knife and we both ..." Melissa did not get to finish her sentence.

"Oh for God's sake, what has all this to do with anything?"

Monica could barely keep the frustration from her voice and was immediately aware of her daughter's sudden uncomfortable silence...her voice was softer when she spoke again...

"I'm sorry Melissa darling but we both think Amy is unwell and...."

"Where is it?"

Michael was standing up from the sofa looking down at his daughter, his gaze then shifted to his wife.

"It's a start Mo, it can't do any harm"

For a while all three were silent exchanging pregnant glances and then as if they had all been waiting for her, Monica sighed heavily and stood up; she held a hand out to Melissa and helped her to her feet. Monica looked at Michael before speaking...

"I suppose we should at least just..."

The sound that took the words from Monica's mouth came from the ceiling above their heads....a loud thump that sent a tiny crack racing along the plaster and caused the repro silver chandelier to jiggle on its flex. The sound came from Amy's room. Michael took the stairs two at a time with Monica just behind, almost tripping in her hurry to catch up with him. Downstairs Melissa sat back down heavily on the sofa, the now ever-present knot of fear in her stomach already tightening. She was standing in the centre of the bed; the front of her long pink nightdress caught up and gathered between her arms at her chest, her hands were clasped palm to palm, her knuckles white and bloodless.

"Leave me alone"

Michael watched his daughter's lips move but it wasn't her voice that issued from them.

"Go away and leave me alone..I warn you"

Monica was now at her husband's back, her hot panting breath on the ice cold skin of the back of his neck, her voice loud in his ear.

"Amy what the hell are you doing...Amy...?"

Monica shouldered her way past her husband; she took two steps towards her daughter but something in the little girl's stare froze her to the spot. And then the child was speaking again.

"Don't come any fucking nearer"

Part Thirteen

And then the room went black. Monica heard the light switch click off a split second after it did and was aware of the rush at her side as Michael lunged forward and made a grab for the tiny girl on the bed. She heard the grunt of forced air from Amy's lungs as her daughter was hefted up and then the sound of heavy footfalls as Michael staggered around the limited space hitting his head and shoulders on the bedroom walls...

"No, no...leave me alone, don't....let me go...let me goooo"

"Amy this is for your own good... we are taking you to..."

Michael's words were swallowed up by his daughters' shouted obscenities.

"Get your hands off me you fucking bastard...you piece of shit.....you fucking..."

A tiny foot caught Monica a glancing blow under her chin, she was pushed back bodily against the door jamb and then Michael and Amy were two struggling shadows silhouetted in the bright light of the landing behind her.

"Amy stop that, stop it now do you hear?" Michael's voice echoed loudly in the confined space of the stairwell as he fought to keep balance as the two of them went almost at a tumble down the stairs. The little girl was hitting the side of his head with a clenched fist and scratching at his face with sharp pointed fingernails, her voice a high pitched feral scream. Monica could only stand rooted to the spot on the landing looking through tear filled eyes at the scene below her, her hands squeezed tightly over her ears, her stomach lurching, she was murmuring to no one in a low inaudible voice, over and over again...

"Amy...please darling stop it..stop it Amy...please darling, stop it..... for mummy..."

And at the foot of the stairs, at the entrance to the lounge, Amy stopped.

It was a while before the echoes of the screaming died away, a while before Michael realised his youngest daughter had completely ceased her struggling. He was standing just inside the lounge, taking in gulps of breath, Amy still clasped tightly in his arms...the room was silent, Melissa was sitting where she had been throughout, staring up at both of them from the sofa, like her mother she had both hands cupped over her ears..

"...it's ok daddy, you can put me down now"
Amy's voice was soft, almost pleading.
"Everything is fine now daddy, I'm fine...
really....put me down.... please".

Michael felt his arms tightened around Amy
before he was aware he was doing it,
something deep within told him to hold on
tight, a subtle change in the little girls
breathing, tension in her spine, her
demeanour...When she did start to struggle
again it was with a renewed rage and he
almost lost his grip, her sudden shriek was a
serrated blade against his eardrums.

"You bitch, you told them, didn't you? You little
fucking bitch"

Melissa was making incoherent sounds,
shaking her head from side to side violently
and backing away with her arms behind her

along the sofa towards the other end of the room and the open kitchen door...

"Amy, Amy...calm down darling...calm down...we are not going to hurt you...calm down..."

Michael was struggling to keep a hold on Amy's wriggling body; he had one arm around her midriff and a hand over a pyjama clad bony shoulder, she was straining to reach her sister, screaming at the top of her voice....

"I'll kill you, you little bitch I'll...."

"Amy"

The loud strident shout from somewhere behind them startled both father and daughter, Michael turned on his heels just as Monica's open palmed hand caught Amy hard across the little girl's face sending a gooey string of blood and saliva spraying from her opened mouth. A silence fell in the lounge and for a moment time stood still, the occupants playing a macabre game of 'statues'. The kitchen door slammed shut, one statue had left the room and the game was over. And from her father's arms Amy stared unblinking at her mother. "You fucking bitch".

*

He had her on her back on the sofa; a hand pressed firmly down on each shoulder, his lower body forced against her legs holding them together and down, trapped between the cushions crevice. A tiny trickle of blood ran from one nostril and her right cheekbone was already showing the grey shadow of a bruise. Her eyes were closed but she was not asleep, the trace of a smile played on her lips. Monica had the receiver in her hand and was barking their address to someone at the other end of the phone. She put the phone down.... "Ten minutes".

Monica went to the front door and opened it... '.in preparation'.. She went back into the lounge and cleared her blurred vision with the backs of both hands...And that's when the sobbing started.

"For Christ's sake Michael, what is wrong with her?"

For a few seconds Melissa stood with her back pressed hard against the kitchen door, the only sound being the thump, thump of her own heart, she put out an arm and reached along the wall for the light switch....*wrong house, Melissa...this isn't your old house this is your new house, the light switch is over there*...And then it did not matter, her eyes were accustomed to dull light of the kitchen...she made her way on tip toe for haste to the corridor at the other side and then past the door to the downstairs toilet...another door gave way to the hall and the stairwell...Melissa went up the stairs two at a time...in Amy's bedroom the light was already on...Amy's bed linen a tangled mess on the floor....Melissa made her way around Amy's crumpled bed to the small bedside cabinet..She pulled open the second drawer down...it was there....the small tortoise shell pill box mummy had given Amy a hundred years ago....Melissa pick the container up and shook it....it was in there....downstairs Amy's eyes flicked open and went straight to the ceiling above Michaels head...She tried desperately to sit up but her father's weight on her shoulders and legs was far too strong....her voice was a spat whisper... "Don't you touch that Melissa, I am warning you...leave that alone you fucking bitch..."

Michael glanced over at his wife still standing at the window.... "Where is that bloody ambulance Mo?

...Melissa leapt over Amy's bed and in two strides was out of the bedroom and onto the landing.... she threw herself down the stairs, the box held tightly in her fist..Amy's scream met her halfway down.... "....I will kill you Melissa; I promise you, I will kill you... Eram quod es, eris quod sum.."

The front door at the bottom of the stairs was open, Melissa fought the urge to run through it, down the garden path, out onto the road...away...away....and then she was in the lounge...her heart pounding in her chest....the metal corners of the tortoise shell pill box digging into the skin of her palm.

Her mother was standing by the window holding the curtain back and staring into the darkness, she turned quickly and stared open mouthed as her eldest daughter burst in through the lounge door...Her father was on the sofa leaning heavily over the writhing thing beneath him that was her sister..And then Amy was talking to her.

"Put it back where you found it Melissa and we can be friends again"

Melissa took a faltering step towards the sofa....all peripheral perception gone.

"Just go back up the stairs Melissa and put it back and all will be fine"

The older girl stopped in the centre of the room and held the hand with the box up to her face; her eyes never leaving her sisters, *people were talking, familiar voices all around....making no sense, just jumbled words....*And then Amy was talking again...

"Melissa, my sweet sister put the medallion back and we will be like we were before...like we will always be....just put the medallion back..."

Melissa smiled and turned back towards the lounge door....*the voices were louder now...but Amy's louder...clearer.*

"That's right Melissa, just put it back...no need for mummy or daddy to..."

Melissa was at the lounge door before she sensed the sudden movement at her back, and heard the piercing scream. A hand grabbed at the back of her pyjama jacket collar almost pulling her off her feet, another went to the wrist of her right hand and a strong shaking movement sent the tortoise shell box flying from her grasp. Michael was on it before the box had time to finish its first bounce on the soft surface of the lounge carpet almost toppling forward with the weight of Amy's body on his back. He straightened up with the little girl scratching at his face and pulling down hard on his hair and began staggering towards the open door. Amy sunk her teeth into the soft flesh of his neck as he pushed his way past a completely stunned and terrified Monica. Outside in the fresh cold of the air of night Michael took the left arm of his tiny daughter in his hand and with a violent twisting and sudden stopping of his upper body threw the little girl from his back to send her flailing through the air to fall heavily on the lawn at his feet.Unencumbered now and standing upright, in one fluid movement he had the tortoise shell box open and the medallion furled in his right hand index finger.To the sounds of Amy's frantic screams, Michael Rowland leant back and with a strength that he hadn't possessed since his days as schoolboy javelin champion year four, he threw the medallion high into the black night sky. The moon's white light caught a glint of gold for a split second...and then just as quickly lost it.

A few days later   ....2006.

"Buongiorno, the little one...the bambina, is she gooda now?"

He was standing at the other side of the gate, a newspaper under one bony arm and a pint of milk in his hand; he lived a few doors down the road, Monica knew that but she did not know his name and he saw it in her quizzical expression.

....*Why is he asking...what does he know?*

"Mi scusi, my name is Ciccio I liva down there"

He gestured with gnarled and sun tanned hands to a small bungalow set back along a narrow path a few metres down the road. Monica smiled; she had seen him walk past the house on several occasions but they had never spoken, just a neighbourly nod, she swapped her car keys to her left hand and proffered her right...*better just keep smiling and be polite...*

"Monica"

He took her hand in his and gave it a light and fleeting squeeze mindful of the rolled newspaper under his arm, she would have felt better if he had returned her smile.

"The bambina I hopa she more better now, that night, the other night, I hear her cry out, I hopa she's better now?"....*oh great...Amy is fine now, all forgotten...back to normal...I don't need reminding...*Monica glanced at her watch involuntarily then forced herself to widen her smile.

"Amy is fine now thank you Mr....Ciccio but I really must...."

...get away from him...Amy is her old self now....just a tantrum really....the doctor agrees, brain scan showed no abnormalities.... maybe a viral infection...keep her under surveillance for a couple of weeks...

The little Italian man on the other side of her fence was not to be shrugged off.

"She a cry out things..La signora Monica"

...Christ, what did this little man hear...how good is his English...how embarrassing...

Monica put a hand on the top bar of the gate but did not make any attempt to push it open, something in the man's voice...in his black, brown eyes....

"I'm sorry Mr Ciccio but I am late for...."

"She knows Italian, the bambina...?"

Monica felt the hairs on the back of her neck bristle....she'd forgotten that...Amy did shout out something that night that did not make sense...something in a foreign language...something Italian maybe...*maybe she does Italian at school Monica...maybe she read it somewhere...maybe its lyrics from one of those horrible boy band songs....wise up for chrissakes*...Monica smiled as sweetly as she could and put more pressure on the gate...he was holding it closed...keeping her 'captive'...

"Look Mr...I don't mean to be rude but I have a very important reason..."

"The bambina ...she shouta nothing nice...La signora Moneeca...something bad..."

Monica's smile was gone, she felt herself pushing at the gate, pushing at the man on the other side....*ok so she swore in Italian, Amy said fuck in Italian, is it worth all this...?*He was speaking again.

"Parla in nostra madre tonge, how do you say...? Bambina she say bad long ago Italian thing...La signora Monica...Bambina she say...."eram quod es, eris quod sum"
Monica stared opened mouth at the man baring her way not comprehending a word of what he was saying...And then he placed a cold bony hand over hers and spoke again...
"...words of what the devil himself once spoke ,'*I was what you are...you will be what I am...*" The Italian man's English this time was perfect.

Part Fourteen

2008

The shadowed walls were bare plaster, pitted and cratered with age, the only decoration being a large wooden crucifix with a string of rope beads dangling haphazardly from the rusted nail holding both in place. Above the open unlit fireplace a lighter square of plaster where many years ago my mother's portrait once hung. In one corner a dark wood bookcase stood with scattered paraphernalia instead of books along its shelves, china and terracotta figures, a few small ornately framed photographs...*sepia ghosts of the past*..and on the top, an old ivory coloured marble cased clock whose hands I knew to be frozen at a quarter passed two without having to get closer to see...in another corner an upturned fruit crate supported a small portable plastic television...*the only concession to the twenty-first century in the room.* The carpet underfoot was threadbare; its edges tasselled and

frayed, the colourless pattern on its surface worn away completely by a million footfalls. The window's thick curtains kept the relentlessly bright midday sun out and the oppressive heat, the flies and the thick aromatic smell of my father's tobacco in. On the large scarred table in the centre of the tiny room, a bottle of uncorked red wine, two greasy smeared glasses, a loaf of dry crusted bread and a single lump of yellowed cheese. *My father had made an effort;* he beckoned me to a cane chair at one side of the table and sat on a ragged armchair opposite ...with a single almost nonchalant wave of his left hand to the scant offerings on the table he bade me eat.

I placed my small travel bag on the floor at my feet and ignoring the *food* I poured wine into one of the glasses and sipped gratefully at its cool dry acidity, my father watching my every move, when he spoke it was obvious he had little if any time for further preamble.

"Donato che hanno come solo il desiderio di essere qui come ho da fare qui mi dara cio che siete venuti a darmi ora...."

I caught little of what the man said, the heat was draining, I was fatigued by my journey and my patience was at an end....

"Speak English father, I have already politely requested you do so"

I could not keep the annoyance from my voice. Benedetto De' Angelis's heavy protracted sigh was loud and carried more than a hint of angry defiance...but when he spoke again it was to be as I had asked.

"Donato, you will give me what you have come here to give me please...I can sense you want to be here as much as I want you to..."I did not let him finish his words and although I had to fight to hide my

indifference my voice still sounded as hollow as the false sentiments it conveyed.

"Giorgio, Ruggero, Lucca and Pio, they all send their best regards father"

A look of deep contrition in the old man's eyes was fleeting but nonetheless there and his hushed unsmiling response in his native tongue hurried, almost perfunctory.

"Naturalmente i miei migliori saluti anche a loro"

Will I give his regards to his sons...of course? I nodded in agreement. A sudden and awkward silence followed catching out the clit clit sound of a hard shelled insect scurrying along a wooden surface somewhere hidden in the shadows.

My father stood up from the chair and, turning on his heels, made his shuffling way to the bookshelf, with a gnarled bony hand he picked up a small brown leather pouch, his tobacco pouch.

He sat down again at the table and through the dull light our eyes met. My disapproving look was wasted on him, he took a withered looking cheroot from the pouch and using matches from the same pouch lit it. It was then, in the burst of bright light from the match that I glimpsed for the first time his trembling hands and wild eyes. He shook the match out and all in the room was momentarily hidden in sudden darkness, as a cloud of sulphur assailed my nostrils, I sensed rather than saw him stand again and with a violent downward stab of his hand he crushed the glowing embers of the cheroot between his fingers and the table's surface. "We have wasted enough time before Donato gives me the medallion..." He was moving now, crouching low and making for the bag at my feet, I snatched it from his groping fingers and brought it up to my chest, knocking over the cane chair as I hurriedly got to my feet. His cry of frustration filled the room...*the wailing of a banshee...* and then the wailing died away and became a string of words breathlessly whispered, spat as threat.

"Donato you do not understand...the medallion...I must have it...give me the medallion now...before it's too late...there are many things you do not understand Donato...many things"

I instinctively took a step back from the advancing skeletal figure in the semi dark as bony arms reached out towards me....reached out for the bag I held tightly in my arms.

"Please give me the medallion Donato..I beg you..."

He had stopped inches from me and a single ray of light from a chink in the curtains illuminated the stark features of his face. I could not help but catch my breath. My father had streams of tears coursing down his cheeks, his eyes were wide, imploring, his hands now held prayer like in front of his chest... and then his voice *was* a prayer....

"If not for my sake Donato then do it for your *sorella,* Abrienne"

 And then there she was, the child that never grew up, never had the chance to grow up. The little girl, il sorella... her long black hair a tangled mess around her face.... singing her childish song and pulling me along in the sand by my skinny arms.....

' Donato, Donato, il mio fratellino dimensi il sedere nudo sulla sabbia e spaventa gli insetti....'

In the darkness of my father's squalid room and thirty five years on I could see as plain as day the sister my youth had forced me to forget,

closed my conscious mind to... simply because to have remembered her would have been far too painful...

'Donato, Donato, il mio fratellino dimena il sedere nudo sulla...'

Abrienne my beautiful little sorella, forgive me. The vision blurred and her face once again faded away into the dust of time...*and then Giorgio was standing there...in his tiny fist he held the bamboo fishing rod, over his shoulder a string of fish their black dead soulless eyes staring up into the heat of the sun... "mummy killed Abrienne...mummy put a blanket over her mouth and killed her...daddy told me...daddy told me mummy will kill us all one day....and then also Giorgio was gone, running up the rock strewn path...the string of dead fish hanging over his back dancing together to the same silent music..*

..at first I could make no sense of the sound, it came from the opposite side of the table, it was a sound that did not belong, a sound for a different time, a different place. He was laughing, my father had slumped back in his chair and was laughing...a joyless cackle that echoed raucously in the oppressive heat of the tiny room...and then his laughter was carrying his words along in a tuneless and cruel aria.

"My parents called me Benedetto, Donato...Benedetto...Do you know what Benedetto means Donato ?

I made no answer to the question; it was obvious I was not invited to.

"Go on Donato...guess Donato...tell me what you think Benedetto means, tell me what fuckin Benedetto means".

He was standing, his body shaking, his hands palm out towards me, inviting me, challenging me.

"Then I will tell you" His hands came up to his chest and his palms pressed together as in prayer...

"To be blessed, it means I am blessed Donato".

This time the laughter cried.

"Oh for sure I have been blessed by Donato my son, I have been blessed by none other than il diavolo himself.

The man opposite me drew an arm across his mouth and then palmed his wet eyes, when he looked at me again it was with a mirthless grin that showed an almost toothless jaw.

"Benedetto De' Angelis is blessed as a murderer, with a murderer for a wife, and sons who would wish for him nothing more than his own death. Again the almost helpless laughter.

"And because he didn't think Benedetto De' Angelis had been blessed enough the il diavolo took his only daughter, what do you think of Donato?"

He reached for the bottle in the middle of the table and with a trembling hand poured wine into his glass; he paused holding the bottle in mid air, his eyes found mine and he must have seen something in them that betrayed me. The laughter was gone leaving no trace.

"Don't you dare pity me Donato, I don't ask for or want your pity"

He poured the wine carelessly; it overflowed the glass and sunk blood red into the table's porous surface.

"I deserve and want no-one's pity"

His eyes had strayed to somewhere hidden in the shadows and for a long while he was silent, when he finally spoke again I could hear in his voice the father I had almost completely forgotten.

"Donato, I will speak to you now as maybe I should have done many years ago, I will tell you about your mother Natalia, I will tell you why she died at my hands, I will tell you about Abrienne, I will tell you all you need to know"

He sat taking the glass up in his hand and draining it in one swallow.

"Maybe you will believe my words, maybe not.."

His eyes found mine and it was as if he were looking into my soul.

"I can only speak them Donato, the rest is up to you"

His eyes went down to the ground at my feet, to the bag and then they were in mine again, deeper than ever.

"Why are you here, do you think Donato? What has brought you to me? Why did you seek out the evil you now know you must deliver?"

His questions were the same questions I had asked myself a thousand times, I had no answers.

"You Donato my son, are il vettore.. a 'carrier'....Natalia your mother was as many are and have been,' l'host', " I beseech you Donato.... place the medallion in my hands now, time is something we have little of".

I placed the bag on the table before me and undid its two buckles; I could feel my father's eyes following my every move. I put a hand inside and at once my fingers touched the ice cold metal. I drew it from the bag and handed it to him.My father took it, walked to my side of the table, bent forward and kissed my forehead. The light from the door blinded me for an instant and then the silhouette of my father's form momentarily blocked it out. I watched him walk a few steps and then the silence of his room told me to follow.

Part Fifteen

We were sitting on the bed, my suitcase and the empty travel bag lay unopened exactly where I had left them, on the floor by the wardrobe.

"Of course I will have to go back in a few days Miranda..the police inquiries, the funeral and everything..."

Miranda was nodding and smiling at me trying to catch my eye, she placed a hand on my shoulder..

"Of course darling...do you want me to come with you?, I could take some...?"

I never gave her time to finish her sentence...

"No, no I'll be fine with..."

With what...? what would I be fine with?...my father killing himself,...placing the piece of metal I gave to him into his mouth and fucking killing himself...

I felt a movement, a shifting of weight on the mattress.

"Well if you're sure hun but I really think you need a...I mean would it be easier for you if ? ..."

Miranda was speaking, asking, her questioning unavoidable like the heavy smoke from one of my father's cheroots.

"If you want to talk about it darling, if you need to tell me anything..I.?"

Again I cut her off in mid sentence....I put my hand on hers and looked deep into her eyes

....and then the hot Italian sun was on my skin and I was back in Frascati... following behind the scurrying figure of my father...Benedetto De' Angelis...I' host...up the narrow sand covered path ...into the hills..The medallion clasped tightly in his withered

hand...."*We called it i diavolo ganasce, which in English means, 'The Devil's Jaws'.*

"Sometimes us kids would stand on the rocky edge and shout swear words just to listen to the echoes, jumping about between the sharp jagged crevices and laughing like idiots"

Miranda made to speak, the frown on her forehead deepened and her lips moved but she said nothing.

"Sometimes we would find huge boulders and throw them in, standing in silence, heads cocked, waiting for the sound that would tell us the stones had reached the bottom..... it never came"

I looked over at my wife and felt the first tremble of emotion tighten in my stomach.

"It was a bottomless pit Miranda, a massive abyss in the Alban Hills with sheer rock walls and nothing in its black hell but snakes and scorpions"

Again Miranda's lips moved but no sound came out.

"He stepped into it Miranda, in front of me he just walked to the edge and fucking stepped into it"

I choked on my words; the tears welling up in my eyes, Miranda put a hand on my shoulder her voice was soft but the look on her face was one of almost total bewilderment. One day I would try to answer her questions, one day, if I ever had the answers to them myself.

Part Sixteen

It had been a long afternoon and his wet foot had long since ceased being annoying, it was now painful. He would make sure to buy new

wellington boots before he came out next time.
The trees at the edges of the field had lost
their shape and were now just black walls
closing
in on him as the light quickly faded. One more
length and he would call
it..*Beep...beep..beep..beep.*
*"Yep they are quite strong and getting closer
together"*
He was talking to himself again. *Beep, beep,
beep, beep.*
His hand reached inside the pouch at his waist
and he drew out his trowel. The coin came
away easily; it hadn't been lying too deeply in
the earth. One side had some letters etched
into it but in this light and covered in wet earth
they were almost impossible to read...
Eram...eris...

No, it would have to wait until he got it home and cleaned it up.

The Author

Kim Clover

I was born 69 years ago in the town of Reading, Berkshire. I was one of six siblings. My family on my mother's side are all from St.Helena. She left the beautiful island in the South Atlantic and made her way to England where she married my father in Reading...something I could never quite bring myself to forgive her for.

I went to a boy's only school and made my money for the tuck shop by writing love letters for my fellow testosteronics (I am sure that word does not exist and if it does not, it should) I left school with 8 R.C.E. passes and a complex that other people actually understood algebra and trigonometry. I was brought up on a council estate so I know how to swear, spit, and make a bloody good clay wanger. I bred mice, kept newts, fished with a bent pin as a hook and rode my bike home with grass stuffed in its tyres due to a puncture. I was always ready to help the local milk man on…clay wanger? You need a nice bit of green willow twig about two feet…metres did not exist then…long. A glob of well kneaded red soggy clay stuck on the end. Bring your arm back and a violent wang sent your glob heaven wise. I am sure you get the picture. I started work as an apprentice engineer, and soon realised I was never going to be an apprentice or an engineer. Living on a council estate meant being a labourer, a painter and decorator or joining the army, so I delivered telegrams for the post office.

Now things are a bit of a blur so please bear with me.

I then worked with explosives, radioactivity, and small rubber seals that were paramount in holding swing fire missiles together. Twelve years with the Ministry of Defence, enough said. Whilst all this happened so did marriage. I discovered reading, writing, English mustard and that white wine goes with fish. We bought a shop in Somerset and were pivotal in rural life, ran a social club and were subjected to an unsociable life. Then we sold fish from a van, all stories in their own right. I dished out human organs for transplant, was no stranger to the mortuary, put up TV satellite systems, and delivered and collected rich people's cars. Stir all this around for half a century sitting by the river bank and the result… 'Return to the Broadwaters' the 'The Calling of the Scales' and 'Anguilla's

Retribution' - The Broadwaters Trilogy...and a follow-up another fishy tale..'Kron' During my time underwater I diversified...(it must have been the lack of oxygen) and what follows is the result. *'The Strange World of Kim'* a number of short stories that crept away from my mind whilst I was looking the other way and demanded to be written.. I hope you enjoy them.

Best wishes, Kim.

Printed in Great Britain
by Amazon

44836524R00198